THE KINGFISHER BOOK OF
CLASSIC ANIMAL STORIES

🐦 KINGFISHER

First published 2008 by Kingfisher
an imprint of Macmillan Children's Books
a division of Macmillan Publishers Limited
20 New Wharf Road, London N1 9RR
Basingstoke and Oxford
Associated companies throughout the world
www.panmacmillan.com

ISBN 978-0-7534-1573-3

1 3 5 7 9 10 8 6 4 2
1TR/0608/SF/UNI/157MA/C

A CIP catalogue record for this book is available from the British Library.

Printed in China

THE KINGFISHER BOOK OF

CLASSIC

ANIMAL

STORIES

KINGFISHER

CONTENTS

FOREWORD

I've always loved animals. I've had cats for as long as I can remember, and they're a constant source of amusement and surprise. Dizzy, now aged 17 and more demanding than ever – she's a real madam, but absolutely adorable – won't drink water from a bowl. It has to be in a glass. When she sits in front of it, paws neatly together, head bent forward, it looks as if she is enjoying a cool lemonade. And, of course, when the water level sinks a little too low, her face is in danger of becoming stuck. Another cat of mine, who sadly disappeared, preferred to jump in the washbasin and drink straight from the tap.

I've always had a passion for wild animals too – elephants, in particular, but cheetahs, lemurs, orang-utans, and lots of others as well. Sometimes it's the sheer size of them that is the fascination. Sometimes it's what they are able to do; for instance, did you know that an elephant can pick up a needle with its trunk, and that there are birds that can sew? And yet we have a disturbingly ambivalent relationship with the animal world. However much we may declare our passion for animals, even our affinity with them, we have carried out the most appalling atrocities against them – and still do – and in many countries we have all but destroyed their natural habitat. Luckily, some sort of balance is maintained by the dedication of people like Joy and George Adamson and Gerald

Durrell, who spend their lives working to conserve animals, as you will discover in the extracts from *Born Free* and *My Family and Other Animals*. And it is nothing short of uplifting when humans and animals live and work together in total harmony, as in *Farmer Boy* and *War Horse*.

When I was asked to compile a collection of classic animal stories, I wanted to cover as wide a range of animal types as possible, in order to celebrate both their extraordinary diversity, and the amazing variety of ways in which they have inspired storytellers through the ages. So here we have stories about pets, farm animals, birds, sea animals and wild animals. Some are true stories; most are fiction. Many are characterised by a strong emotional content, just as they might be if they revolved around people. Others are distinguished by their humour. In some, such as *The Hodgeheg* and *Mrs Frisby and the Rats of Nimh*, the animals talk. In others, such as *The Incredible Journey*, they are silent, and it is the writer's skill which allows us to understand the impact of what is happening in their lives. All of them have been chosen because they represent the most talented authors writing at the height of their ability, in homage to our furry and feathered friends.

Sally Grindley

INTRODUCTION

Nobody really knows who Aesop was, nor even when he lived.
The most popular theory is that he was a Greek slave who lived
in the 6th century BC. *All we can be sure of is that his fables*
(or fables attributed to him) are known and loved all over the
world. Expressions born out of them are part of our everyday
language – "sour grapes", "don't count your chickens before
they're hatched", "a wolf in sheep's clothing", and so on. Stories
such as The Hare and the Tortoise, The Lion and the Mouse
and The Town Mouse and the Country Mouse *are full of*
wit and cunning. These fables provide morality lessons about
the wise and foolish behaviour of humans, made palatable
because of the entertaining way they are told.
The Jay and the Peacocks *is no exception.*

AESOP'S FABLES

RETOLD BY SAVIOUR PIROTTA

The Jay and the Peacocks

In the branches of an ancient oak tree, there was a nest made from twigs and leaves, held together with straw and wool. In it lived a mother and father jay, and their four children, who cheeped and chirped happily all day long. When the little jays were big enough to fly, their mama and papa showed them how to catch their own worms, and how to imitate other birds for fun, a marvellous talent which all jays are blessed with.

When the biggest jay was seven weeks old, and nearly a grown-up, he flew over a tall hedge and found himself in a king's garden. It was late spring and the roses were already in bloom. There was a fountain in the middle of the garden, with a host of magnificent peacocks lazing on the grass around it.

The young jay had never seen such dazzling creatures before.

The peacocks paraded in front of the fountain, their glossy tails fanned out to catch the light of the sun. Their feathers sparkled and shimmered, a sea of blue and green flecked with gold and jet. Suddenly the jay felt embarrassed about his own humble plumage, like a man who blunders into a temple wearing his everyday rags in a nightmare. The jay hid in a fig tree.

A servant came out of the palace with a wicker basket and scattered food for the peacocks. A young prince ran out to play among the birds, laughing and admiring their colours. After they had eaten, the peacocks all fell asleep and the jay was able to flutter out of the tree unnoticed. Back home, his mother asked if he'd had a good day.

"It was fine," he said, but without his usual enthusiasm, and all that night he could not sleep for thinking about those peacocks and their gorgeous feathers. In the morning, he flew to a pond and, inspecting his sad reflection in the water, sighed, "Oh, how I wish I was a peacock too. Then I could live by the fountain in the king's garden and be admired by the prince. It would be much more fun than hunting for acorns or looking for worms."

From then on, he took to hiding in the fig tree every day, watching and envying the peacocks in the garden.

"Come away," said his brothers and sisters when they discovered his secret. "There are lambs in the field and we have learned to bleat like them. It's much more fun than hiding in this tree."

"Come away from that garden," said his mother when the young jays told her all about it. "The countryside is teeming with insects for us to catch and eat."

"Come away from that tree," said the jay's father, when the jay's mother told him why he did not spend time with his family any more. "I'll show you how to dig holes in the earth so that you may know where to hide acorns when they ripen."

But nothing could lure the young jay away from the king's garden. Spring turned to summer and the peacocks started to moult, dropping feathers on the grass. The jay had an idea. "Here's my chance to become a peacock," he said to himself. And, while the peacocks were asleep in the shade of a rose-covered pergola, he hopped down from his perch and collected the fallen feathers. Before long, he had enough to carry out his plan. He found a piece of straw that had blown into a hedge and, using his claws and beak, tied the peacock feathers to his own tail.

"Now I am a peacock too," he said happily. And he flew proudly on to the newly cut grass.

"Hello there."

One by one the peacocks lifted their heads and blinked their jewel-like eyes.

"Oh look, brothers, there's a new peacock in the garden," said one. "Are you a new gift for the prince? Who sent you? The ruler of wondrous Babylon? The pharaoh of mysterious Egypt?"

They all crowded round to welcome him, setting up a terrible din. Then something unexpected and disastrous happened. With all the hugging and pushing and shoving, the straw that bound the peacock feathers to the jay's tail came loose. The feathers fell off.

"What treachery is this?" shrieked one of the peacocks. "You are not a peacock at all, but a common bird, fit only to live in the woods. You stole those feathers from us. Give them back, you thief!"

The other peacocks, angry at being tricked, started to peck the jay, and soon he had lost all the peacock feathers, as well as many of his own. The poor bird only just managed to escape with his life. After regaining his breath in the fig tree, he limped sadly home.

His mother and father did not scold him for being so foolish. They fed him fat juicy worms while he recovered. When he got better, his father showed him how to hide acorns when they ripened. The jay had great fun learning to call out like other birds and imitating the sounds of cats and lambs. He never envied those dreadful peacocks again, but was quite happy just to be himself.

The moral of the story is: fine feathers don't make a fine bird!

INTRODUCTION

This is one of Rudyard Kipling's much-loved Just So Stories, *which he wrote for his daughter, Effie, and published in 1902. Each of the stories tells very fancifully how an animal became the way it is. I chose this particular story because I love the ridiculous notion of a man jumping up and down inside a whale and giving it hiccoughs. I also love the ingenuity of the man (and Kipling!), who uses his suspenders and raft to build a grate that will lodge in the whale's throat, thus preventing it from swallowing anything big ever again. Kipling's joyful use of language in all of his* Just So Stories *is a real treat.*

JUST SO STORIES

RUDYARD KIPLING

How the Whale Got His Throat

In the sea, once upon a time, O my Best Beloved, there was a
Whale, and he ate fishes. He ate the starfish and the garfish, and
the crab and the dab, and the plaice and the dace, and the skate
and his mate, and the mackereel and the pickereel, and the really
truly twirly-whirly eel. All the fishes he could find in all the sea
he ate with his mouth – so! Till at last there was only one small
fish left in all the sea, and he was a small 'Stute Fish, and he swam
a little behind the Whale's right ear, so as to be out of harm's way.

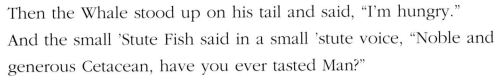

Then the Whale stood up on his tail and said, "I'm hungry."
And the small 'Stute Fish said in a small 'stute voice, "Noble and
generous Cetacean, have you ever tasted Man?"

"No," said the Whale. "What is it like?"

"Nice," said the small 'Stute Fish. "Nice but nubbly."

"Then fetch me some," said the Whale, and he made the sea
froth up with his tail.

"One at a time is enough," said the 'Stute Fish. "If you swim to
latitude Fifty North, longitude Forty West (that is magic), you will
find, sitting on a raft, in the middle of the sea, with nothing on but
a pair of blue canvas breeches, a pair of suspenders (you must not
forget the suspenders, Best Beloved), and a jackknife, one
shipwrecked Mariner, who, it is only fair to tell you, is a man of
infinite-resource-and-sagacity."

So the Whale swam and swam to latitude Fifty North, longitude
Forty West, as fast as he could swim, and on a raft, in the middle of
the sea, with nothing to wear except a pair of blue canvas breeches,
a pair of suspenders (you must particularly remember the
suspenders, Best Beloved), and a jackknife, he found one single,
solitary shipwrecked Mariner, trailing his toes in the water. (He had
his mummy's leave to paddle, or else he would never have done it,
because he was a man of infinite-resource-and-sagacity.)

Then the Whale opened his mouth back and back and back till
it nearly touched his tail, and he swallowed the shipwrecked
Mariner, and the raft he was sitting on, and his blue canvas
breeches, and the suspenders (which you must not forget), and the
jackknife – He swallowed them all down into his warm, dark,
inside cupboards, and then he smacked his lips – so, and turned
round three times on his tail.

But as soon as the Mariner, who was a man of infinite-resource-
and-sagacity, found himself truly inside the Whale's warm, dark,

inside cupboards, he stumped and he jumped
and he thumped and he bumped, and he
pranced and he danced, and he banged
and he clanged, and he hit and he bit,
and he leaped and he creeped, and
he prowled and he howled, and
he hopped and he dropped, and he
cried and he sighed, and he crawled
and he bawled, and he stepped and
he lepped, and he danced
hornpipes where he shouldn't,

and the Whale felt most unhappy indeed. (Have you forgotten the suspenders?)

So he said to the 'Stute Fish, "This man is very nubbly, and besides he is making me hiccough. What shall I do?"

"Tell him to come out," said the 'Stute Fish.

So the Whale called down his own throat to the shipwrecked Mariner, "Come out and behave yourself. I've got the hiccoughs."

"Nay, nay!" said the Mariner. "Not so, but far otherwise. Take me to my natal-shore and the white-cliffs-of-Albion, and I'll think about it." And he began to dance more than ever.

"You had better take him home," said the 'Stute Fish to the Whale. "I ought to have warned you that he is a man of infinite-resource-and-sagacity."

So the Whale swam and swam and swam, with both flippers and his tail, as hard as he could for the hiccoughs; and at last he saw the Mariner's natal-shore and the white-cliffs-of-Albion, and he rushed halfway up the beach, and opened his mouth wide and wide and wide, and said, "Change here for Winchester, Ashuelot, Nashua, Keene, and stations on the Fitchburg Road"; and just as he said "Fitch", the Mariner walked out of his mouth. But while the Whale had been swimming, the Mariner, who was indeed a person of infinite-resource-and-sagacity, had taken his jackknife and cut up the raft into a little square grating all running criss-cross, and he had tied it firm with his suspenders (now you know why you were not to forget the suspenders!), and he dragged that grating good and tight into the Whale's throat, and there it stuck! Then he recited the following Sloka, which, as you have not heard it, I will now proceed to relate –

By means of a grating
I have stopped your ating.

For the Mariner he was also an Hi-ber-ni-an. And he stepped out on the shingle, and went home to his mother, who had given him leave to trail his toes in the water; and he married and lived happily ever afterward. So did the Whale. But from that day on, the grating in his throat, which he could neither cough up nor swallow down, prevented him eating anything except very, very small fish; and that is the reason why whales nowadays never eat men or boys or little girls. The small 'Stute Fish went and hid himself in the mud under the Doorsills of the Equator. He was afraid that the Whale might be angry with him.

The Whale never found the little 'Stute Fish till he got over his temper, and then they became good friends again.

The Sailor took the jackknife home. He was wearing the blue canvas breeches when he walked out on the shingle. The suspenders were left behind, you see, to tie the grating with; and that is the end of that tale.

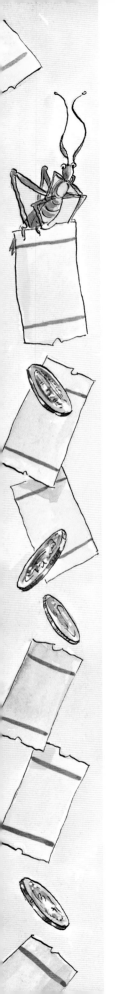

INTRODUCTION

Who would have thought you could write a story about the friendship and adventures of a boy, a cricket, a mouse and a cat? Well, that's just what George Selden did, and it became a classic. Mario, the boy, helps his parents run a newsstand in the Times Square subway station. He adopts a cricket, called Chester, who has taken up residence at the station, as do Tucker Mouse and Harry Cat, regular night-time visitors to the stand when it is closed. Between them all, they introduce Chester to New York. Though he is a country cricket, Chester begins to enjoy his new life. He particularly enjoys the matchbox home Mario has made for him, so, when the boy buys him an elaborate palace to sleep in, Chester is happy to let Tucker take it over . . .

THE CRICKET IN
TIMES SQUARE

GEORGE SELDEN

Chester Cricket was having a dream. In his dream he was
sitting on top of his stump back in Connecticut, eating a leaf
from the willow tree. He would bite off a piece of leaf, chew it up
and swallow it, but for some reason it didn't taste as good as
usual. There was something dry and papery about it, and it had a
bitter flavour. Still Chester kept eating, hoping that it would begin
to taste better.

A storm came up in his dream. The wind blew clouds of dust
across the meadow. They swirled around his stump, and Chester
began to sneeze because the dust got in his nose. But he still held

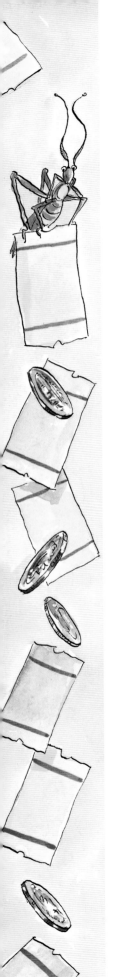

on to the leaf. And then he sneezed such a big sneeze that it woke him up.

Chester looked around him. He had been walking in his sleep and he was sitting on the edge of the cash register. The storm had been a gust of air that blew into the newsstand when the shuttle pulled up to the station. He was still choking from the dirt that flew around him. Chester looked down at his two front legs, half expecting to find the willow leaf. But it was no leaf he was holding. It was a two dollar bill and he had already eaten half of it.

He dropped the bill and leaped over to the cricket cage, where Tucker Mouse was sleeping peacefully. Chester shook the silver bell furiously; it rang like a fire alarm. Tucker jumped out from under his blanket of dollar bills and ran around the cage shouting, "Help! Fire! Murder! Police!"

Then he realized where he was and sat down panting. "What is the matter with you, Chester?" he said. "I could have died from fright."

"I just ate half of a two dollar bill," said Chester.

Tucker stared at him with disbelief. "You did what?" he asked.

"Yes," said Chester, "look." He fetched the ruined two dollar bill from the cash register. "I dreamed it was a leaf and I ate it."

"Oh oh oh oh," moaned Tucker Mouse. "Not a one dollar bill – not even a one dollar bill and a fifty cent piece – two dollars you had to eat! And from the Bellinis too – people who hardly make two dollars in two days."

"What am I going to do?" asked Chester.

"Pack your bags and go to California," said Tucker.

Chester shook his head. "I can't," he said. "They've been so good to me – I can't run away."

Tucker Mouse shrugged his shoulders. "Then stay and take the rap," he said. He crept out of the cage and examined the remains of the money. "There's still half of it left. Maybe we could put scotch tape along the edge and pass it off as a one dollar bill."

"No one would believe it," said Chester. He sat down, still forlornly holding the bill. "Oh dear – and things were going along so nicely."

Tucker Mouse put his bedclothes back in the cash register drawer and came to sit beside Chester. "Buck up," he said. "We could still figure something out, maybe."

They both concentrated for a minute. Then Tucker clapped his paws and squeaked, "I got it! Eat the rest of it and they'll never know what happened."

"They'd accuse each other of losing it," said Chester. "I don't want to make any bad feeling between them."

"Oh, you're so honourable!" said Tucker. "It's disgusting."

"Besides, it tastes bad," added Chester.

"Then how about this," Tucker had a new idea. "We frame the janitor who cleans the station. I'll take the evidence over and plant

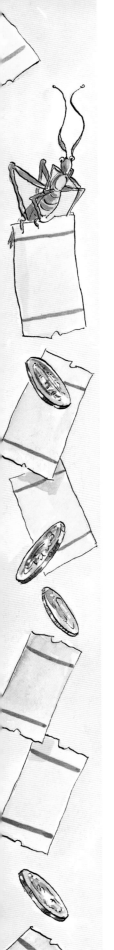

it in his water closet. He whopped me with a mop last week. I would be glad to see him go to jail for a few days."

"No, no," said Chester. "We can't get somebody else in trouble."

"Then a stranger," said Tucker. "We tip over the Kleenex, break the glass in the alarm clock and throw all the small change on the floor. They'll think a thief came in the night. You could even put a bandage on and make out like a hero. I could see it all—"

"No!" Chester interrupted him. "The damage we'd do would cost even more than the two dollars."

Tucker had one more idea: he was going to volunteer to go over and swipe two dollars from the lunch counter. But before he could suggest that, the top of the stand was suddenly lifted off. They had forgotten what time it was. Mama Bellini, who was on duty in the morning, stood towering, frowning down on them. Tucker let out a squeak of fear and jumped to the floor.

"Catch the mouse!" shouted Mama. She picked up a *Fortune* magazine – very big and heavy – and heaved it after Tucker. It hit him on the left hind leg just as he vanished into the drain pipe.

Chester Cricket sat frozen to the spot. He was caught redhanded, holding the chewed-up two dollars in his front legs. Muttering with rage, Mama Bellini picked him up by his antennae, tossed him into the cricket cage and locked the gate behind him. When she had put the newsstand in order, she pulled out her knitting and began to work furiously. But she was so angry she kept dropping stitches, and that made her angrier still.

Chester crouched in a far corner of the cage. Things had been going so well between Mama and him – but that was all ruined now. He half expected that she would pick him up, cage and all, and throw him onto the shuttle tracks.

At eight-thirty, Mario and Pap arrived. Mario wanted to go to Coney Island for a swim today, but Mama Bellini stretched out her hand and pointed sternly at Chester. There he was, with the evidence beside him.

A three-cornered conversation began. Mama denounced Chester as a money eater and said further that she suspected him of inviting mice and other unsavoury characters into the newsstand at night. Papa said he didn't think Chester had eaten the two dollars on purpose, and what difference did it make if a mouse or two came in? Mama said he had to go. Papa said he could stay, but he'd have to be kept in the cage. And Mario knew that Chester, like all people who were used to freedom, would rather die than live his life behind bars.

Finally it was decided that since the cricket was Mario's pet, the boy would have to replace the money. And when he had, Chester could come out again. Until then – the cage.

By working part time delivering groceries, when he wasn't taking care of the newsstand, Mario thought he could earn enough in a couple of weeks to get Chester out of jail. Of course that would mean no swimming at Coney Island, and no movies, and no nothing, but it was worth it. He fed the cricket his breakfast – left over asparagus tips and a piece of cabbage leaf. Chester had practically no appetite after what had happened. Then, when the cricket was finished, Mario said, "Goodbye," and told him not to worry, and went off to the grocery store to see about his job.

That night, after Papa had shut up the newsstand, Chester was hanging through the gilded bars of his cage. Earlier in the evening Mario had come back to feed him his supper, but then he had to leave right away to get in a few more hours of work. Most of the day Chester had spent inventing hopping games to try to keep himself entertained, but they didn't work, really. He was bored and lonely. The funny thing was that although he had been sleepy and

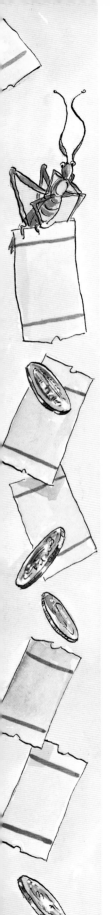

kept wishing it were night, now that it was, he couldn't fall asleep.

Chester heard the soft padding of feet beneath him. Harry Cat sprang up and landed on the shelf. In a moment Tucker Mouse followed him from the stool, groaning with pain. He was still limping in his left hind leg where the *Fortune* magazine had hit him.

"How long is the sentence?" asked Harry.

"Until Mario can pay back the money," sighed Chester.

"Couldn't you get out on bail for the time being?" asked Tucker.

"No," said Chester. "And anyway, nobody has any bail. I'm surprised they let me off that easily."

Harry Cat folded his front paws over each other and rested his head on them. "Let me get this straight," he said. "Does Mario have to work for the money as punishment – or does he just have to get it somewhere?"

"He just has to get it," said Chester. "Why should he be punished? I'm the one who ate the money."

Harry looked at Tucker – a long look, as if he expected the mouse to say something. Tucker began to fidget. "Say, Chester, you want to escape?" he asked. "We can open the cage. You could come and live in the drain pipe."

"No," Chester shook his head. "It wouldn't be fair to Mario. I'll just have to serve out the time."

Harry looked at Tucker again and began tapping one of his paws. "Well?" he said finally.

Tucker moaned and massaged his sore spot. "Oh, my poor leg! That Mama Bellini can sure heave a magazine. Feel the bump, Harry," he offered.

"I felt it already," said Harry. "Now enough of the stalling. You have money."

"Tucker has money?" said Chester Cricket.

Tucker looked nervously from one to the other. "I have my life

savings," he said in a pathetic voice.

"He's the richest mouse in New York," said Harry. "Old Money Bags Mouse, he's known as."

"Now wait a minute, Harry," said Tucker. "Let's not make too much from a few nickels and dimes."

"How did you get money?" asked Chester.

Tucker Mouse cleared his throat and began wringing his two front feet. When he spoke, his voice was all choked up with emotion. "Years ago," he said, "when yet a little mouse I was, tender in age and lacking in experience, I moved from the sweet scenes of my childhood – Tenth Avenue, that is – into the Times Square subway station. And it was here that I learned the value of economicness – which means saving. Many and many an old mouse did I see, crawling away unwanted to a poor mouse's grave, because he had not saved. And I resolved that such a fate would never come to me."

"All of which means that you've got a pile of loot back there in the drain pipe," said Harry Cat.

"Just a minute, please, if you wouldn't mind," said Tucker. "I'll tell it in my own way." His voice became high and pitiful again. "So for all the long years of my youth, when I could have been gambolling – which means playing – with the other mousies, I saved. I saved paper, I saved food, I saved clothing—"

"Save time and get to the point," said Harry.

Tucker gave Harry a sour smile. "And I also saved money," he went on. "In the course of many years of scrounging, it was only natural I should find a certain amount of loose change. Often – oh, often, my friends," Tucker put his hand over his heart, "would I sit in the opening of my drain pipe, watching the human beings and waiting. And whenever one of them dropped a coin – however small! – pennies, I love – I would dash out, at great peril

to life and limb, and bring it back to my house. Ah, when I think
of the tramping shoes and the dangerous galoshes—! Many times
have I had my toes stepped on and my whiskers torn off because
of these labours. But it was worth it! Oh, it was worth it, my
friends, on account of now I have two half dollars, five quarters,
two dimes, six nickels and eighteen pennies tucked away in the
drain pipe!"

"Which makes two dollars and ninety-three cents," said Harry
Cat, after doing some quick addition.

"And proud I am of it!" said Tucker Mouse.

"If you've got all that, why did you want to sleep on the two
dollar bills in the cricket cage?" asked Chester.

"No folding money yet," said Tucker. "It was a new sensation."

"You can get Chester out and still have ninety-three cents left,"
said Harry Cat.

"But I'll be ruined," whimpered Tucker. "I'll be wiped out. Who
will take care of me in my old age?"

"I will!" said Harry. "Now stop acting like a skinflint and let's
get the money."

Chester rang the silver bell to get their attention. "I don't think
Tucker should have to give up his life savings," he said. "It's his
money and he can do what he wants with it."

Tucker Mouse poked Harry in the ribs. "Listen to the cricket,"
he said. "Acting noble and making me look like a bum. Of course
I'll give the money! Wherever mice are spoken of, never let it be
said that Tucker Mouse was stingy with his worldly goods.
Besides, I could think of it as rent I pay for sleeping in the cage."
In order that Tucker could keep at least one of each kind of coin,
Harry Cat figured out that they should bring over one half dollar,
four quarters, one dime, five nickels and fifteen cents. That
would leave the mouse with a half dollar, a quarter, a dime, a

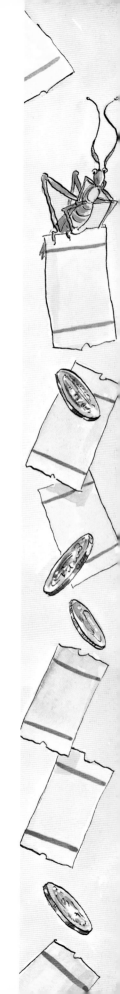

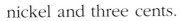

nickel and three cents.

"It's not a bad beginning," said Tucker. "I could make up the losses in a year, maybe."

The cat and the mouse had to make several trips back and forth between the drain pipe and the newsstand, carrying the money in their mouths. They passed the coins into the cage one by one, and Chester built them up into a column, starting with the half dollar on the bottom and ending with the dime, which was smallest, on top. It was morning by the time they were finished. They had just time enough to share half of a hot dog before Mama Bellini was due to open the stand.

Mario came with her. He wanted to feed Chester early and then work all morning until he took over the newsstand at noon. When

they lifted off the cover, Mama almost dropped her end. There was Chester, sitting on top of the column of change, chirping merrily.

Mama's first suspicion was that the cricket had sneaked out and smuggled all the money from the cash register into the cage. But when she looked in the drawer, the money from the night before was still there.

Mario had the idea that Papa might have left it as a surprise. Mama shook her head. She would certainly have known if he had two dollars to leave anybody.

They asked Paul, the conductor, if he'd seen anyone around the newsstand. He said no. The only thing he'd noticed was that that big cat who sometimes prowled through the station had seemed to be busier than usual last night. And of course they knew that he couldn't have had anything to do with replacing the money.

But whoever left it, Mama Bellini was good to her word. Chester was allowed out of the cage, and no further questions were asked. Although she wouldn't have admitted it for the world, Mama felt the same way about money that Tucker Mouse did. When you had it, you had it – and you didn't bother too much about where it came from.

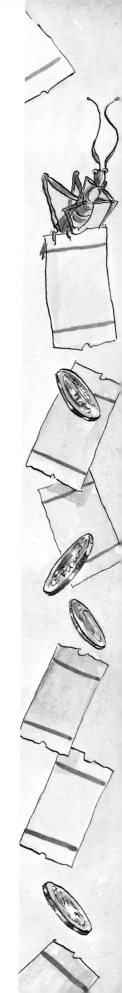

INTRODUCTION

There are many theories about where the Brer Rabbit *stories originated. It seems to be the case that they derived from both African Bantu and Cherokee Indian sources. Brer Rabbit himself, the ultimate trickster, became a central figure in the 'Uncle Remus' stories written by Joel Chandler Harris in the late nineteenth century. He set the stories in the state of Georgia in the southern United States, where 'brer' is slang for 'brother'. The pranks played by Brer Rabbit and Brer Fox, and the attempts by other animals to outwit them, never fail to amuse. This is one of the funniest.*

BRER FOX CATCHES OLD MAN TARRYPIN

JOEL CHANDLER HARRIS

RETOLD BY S. E. SCHLOSSER

Well now, Brer Rabbit had made friends with Old Man Tarrypin, a big turtle that lived in the pond near his house. Brer Rabbit and Old Man Tarrypin liked to pull tricks on Brer Fox, and that rascally fellow got pretty mad about it.

Since he couldn't catch Brer Rabbit nohow, Brer Fox decided that he'd get even with Old Man Tarrypin instead. He started walking beside the pond every day, hoping to find the turtle out of the water.

One morning, as he was taking his daily stroll, Brer Fox saw Old Man Tarrypin sitting right in the centre of the road. The old turtle looked hot and bothered about something. He kept shaking his head back and forth and he was panting like he was out of breath.

"Howdy, Brer Tarrypin," said Brer Fox, stopping beside the old turtle. "What's the matter wid you?"

"I was a-strolling in the field beside my pond when the farmer came along and set it on fire," Old Man Tarrypin gasped. "I had to run and run, but that ol' fire was faster than me, so I curled up in my shell while it passed right over me! My shell is hotter than the noon-day sun, and I think I done singed my tail!"

"Let me have a look," said Brer Fox. So Old Man Tarrypin

uncurled his tail and poked it out of his shell. Immediately, Brer Fox grabbed him by the tail and swung him right off the ground.

"I gotcha now, Brer Tarrypin," cried Brer Fox. "You ain't gonna bother me no more!"

Brer Fox swung the poor old turtle back and forth by his tail, trying to decide what to do. Putting Old Man Tarrypin into the fire was a tempting idea, but then he remembered how the old turtle had curled up into his shell so the fire couldn't touch him. Brer Fox frowned. Fire was no good, then.

Brer Fox decided to drown Old Man Tarrypin instead. He tucked the turtle under his arm and carried him down to the springhouse by the pond.

Well, Old Man Tarrypin begged and begged Brer Fox not to drown him. He'd rather go back into the fire in the field on account of he'd kind of gotten used to being burned.

"Please, oh please don't drown me," Old Man Tarrypin begged.

"I ain't making no promises," Brer Fox retorted. "You've played too many tricks on me, Brer Tarrypin."

Brer Fox thrust him into the water and began bouncing him up and down.

"Oh, I is drowning," shouted Old Man Tarrypin when his head bounced out of the water. "Don't let go of my tail, Brer Fox, or I'll be drowned for sure!"

"That's the idea, Brer Tarrypin," Brer Fox yelled back and let go of his tail.

Immediately, Old Man Tarrypin splashed down and down into the water and thumped onto the mud on the bottom, kerplicky-splat.

That's when Brer Fox remembered that Old Man Tarrypin lived in the pond, and there was never any fear of him drowning, nohow! He could hear him laughing from the bottom of the pond: "I-dare-ya-ta-come-down-'ere."

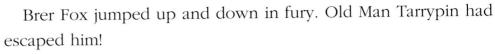

Brer Fox jumped up and down in fury. Old Man Tarrypin had escaped him!

From the other side of the pond, Brer Bull Frog called out, "Knee-deep! Knee-deep!"

Brer Fox glared at the pond, and then looked back at Brer Bull Frog. "It's only knee-deep?" he asked suspiciously.

"Knee-deep, knee-deep!" Brer Bull Frog said again.

All the little frogs joined in the chorus then. "Better-believe-it! Better-believe-it!"

Well, thought Brer Fox, if it was only knee-deep, then he'd have no trouble catching Old Man Tarrypin.

"Wade-in, wade-in!" croaked Brer Bull Frog.

"Knee-deep, knee-deep!" agreed all the little frogs.

Brer Fox didn't much like water, but he really wanted to catch Old Man Tarrypin. He approached the edge of the pond cautiously. From underneath the water, Old Man Tarrypin laughed at him, and his words bubbled up to Brer Fox, "I-dare-ya-ta-come-down-'ere! I-dare-ya-ta-come-down-'ere!"

Well. That did it. Brer Fox ran right up to the edge of the pond. Leaning over, he looked into the water and saw another fox staring at him.

"Dat's-your-brother! Dat's-your-brother," Brer Bull Frog told Brer Fox.

Brer Fox was thrilled. He didn't know he had a brother. Now that there were two foxes, catching Old Man Tarrypin would be a cinch! Brer Fox leaned down to shake hands with his newfound brother, and toppled right down into the deep water of the pond.

All of the frogs laughed and laughed at the trick they had played on Brer Fox, and Old Man Tarrypin started swimming up from the bottom of the pond, his red eyes fixed on Brer Fox's tail. Brer Fox knew that the old turtle wanted to pull him down under

that water and drown him, so he learned to swim mighty quick! With much splashing and squirming and kicking, Brer Fox made it to the edge of the pond, where he jumped out and ran away as fast as he could, while Brer Bull Frog laughed and the little frogs shouted with glee.

The last thing he heard as he rounded the corner was the voice of Old Man Tarrypin calling, "I-dare-ya-ta-come-down-'ere."

Brer Fox never messed with Old Man Tarrypin again.

INTRODUCTION

Mrs Frisby and her family of field mice spend the winter in a vegetable garden belonging to a farmer. At the beginning of March, it's vital for them to flee the garden before the farmer sets about it with his plough. But Mrs Frisby's youngest son, Timothy, has fallen dangerously ill with pneumonia and, according to the doctor, should not be moved, especially to anywhere cold. The family's summer nest will not have had a chance to warm up. All Mrs Frisby can hope is that 'moving day' will be delayed by a sudden cold snap or rain . . .

MRS FRISBY AND THE RATS OF NIMH

ROBERT C. O'BRIEN

Mr Fitzgibbon's Plough

When Mrs Frisby went into her house, she found Timothy asleep and the other children waiting, frightened, sad and subdued.

"He went to sleep right after you left," Teresa said. "He's waked up twice, and the second time he wasn't delirious. He said his chest hurt and his head hurt. But, Mother, he seemed so weak – he could hardly talk. He asked where you were, and I told him. Then he went back to sleep."

Mrs Frisby went to where Timothy lay, a small ball of damp fur curled under a bit of cloth blanket. He looked scarcely larger than he had when she and Mr Frisby had carried him to Mr Ages as an infant, and the thought of that trip made her wish Mr Frisby were alive to reassure the children and tell them not to worry. But he

was not, and it was she who must say it.

"Don't worry," she said. "Mr Ages gave me some medicine for him and says he will recover." She mixed the contents of one of the packets, a grey-green powder, in water, and then gently shook Timothy awake.

He smiled. "You're back," he said in a voice as small as a whisper.

"I'm back, and I've brought you some medicine. Mr Ages says it will make you all right." She lifted his head on her arm, and he swallowed the medicine. "I expect it's bitter," she said.

"It's not so bad," he said. "It tastes like pepper." And he fell back to sleep immediately.

The next morning, as predicted, his fever was lower, his breathing grew easier, and his heartbeat slowed down; still, that day he slept seven hours out of each eight. The next day he stayed awake longer, and on the third day had no fever at all, just as Mr Ages has said. However, since Mr Ages had been right in all that, Mrs Frisby knew he was sure to have been right in the other things he had said: Timothy was not really strong yet. He must stay in bed, stay warm, and breathe only warm air.

During those three days she had stayed close by his side, but on the fourth she felt cheerful enough to go for a walk, and also to fetch some more of the corn from the stump so they could have it for supper.

She went out of her front door into the sunshine and was surprised to find a spring day waiting for her. The weather had turned warm while she had stayed indoors; February was over and March had come in, as they say, like a lamb. There was a smell of dampness in the air as the frosted ground thawed, a smell of things getting ready to grow. It made her feel even more cheerful than before, and she walked almost gaily across the garden.

And yet despite the fine warmth of the day – indeed, in a way,

because of it – Mrs Frisby could not quite get rid of a nagging worry that kept flickering in her mind; it was the kind of worry that, if you push it out of this corner of your thoughts, pops up in that corner, and finally in the middle, where it has to be faced. It was the thought of Moving Day.

Everybody knows that the ground hog comes up from the deep hole where he was slept away the winter, looks around, and if he decides the cold weather is not over, goes back down to sleep for another six weeks. Field mice like Mrs Frisby are not so lucky. When winter is over, they must move out of the garden and back to the meadow or the pasture. For as soon as the weather allows, Farmer Fitzgibbon's tractor comes rumbling through, pulling the sharp-bladed plough through the soil, turning over every foot of it. No animal caught in the garden that day is likely to escape alive, and all the winter homes, all the tunnels and holes and nests and cocoons, are torn up. After the plough comes the harrow, with its heavy creaking discs, and then the people with hoes and seeds.

Not all the field mice move into the garden for the winter, of course. Some find their way to barn lofts; some even creep into people's houses and live under the eaves or in attics, taking their chances with mousetraps. But the Frisbys had always come to the garden, preferring the relative safety and freedom of the outdoors.

Moving Day therefore depends on the weather, and that is why a fine day set Mrs Frisby worrying, even as she enjoyed it. As soon as the frost was out of the ground, the plough would come, and that could happen as much as a month earlier (or later) one year than the last.

And the worry was this: if it came too soon, Timothy would not be able to move. He was supposed to stay in bed, and moving meant a long walk across the field of winter wheat, up and down the hill to the brook's edge, where the Frisbys made their summer home. Not only that – the home itself would be damp and chilly for the first few weeks (as summer houses always are) until early spring turned to late spring and the nights grew truly warm. This was something that Mrs Frisby and the children did not ordinarily mind; Moving Day, in fact, was normally a gay time, for it marked the end of the grey weather and the frost. It was like the beginning of a summer holiday.

But this year? Now that Mrs Frisby had faced the problem, she did not see any answer except to hope that the day would not come too early. In another month (according to Mr Ages), Timothy would be strong enough. Perhaps she was only borrowing trouble. One warm day, she told herself, does not make a summer. No, nor even a spring.

She walked on through the garden and saw ahead of her a small figure she knew. It was a lady shrew, a tiny thing scarcely bigger than a peanut, but with a wit as sharp as her teeth. She lived in a simple hole in the ground a few yards away; Mrs Frisby met her often and had grown to like her, though shrews are generally unpopular, having a reputation for short tempers and extremely large appetites.

"Good morning," said Mrs Frisby.

"Ah, Mrs Frisby. Good morning indeed. Too good is what I'm thinking." The shrew was holding a stalk of straw, which she now thrust into the earth. It went down easily for two inches or more before it bent in her hand. "Look at that. The top of the frost is gone already. Another few days like this, and it will be all gone. Then we will have the tractor in here again, breaking everything up."

"So soon? Do you really think so?" asked Mrs Frisby, her worry returning in a rush, stronger than before.

"He ploughs when the frost is gone. Remember the spring of sixty-five? That year he ploughed on the eleventh day of March,

and on a Sunday at that. I moved down to the woods that night and nearly froze to death in a miserable hollow log. And that day came after a week of days just like this."

Mrs Frisby did remember it; her family, too, had shivered through those chilly nights. For the fact was, the earlier Moving Day came, the colder the nights were likely to be.

"Oh, dear," she said. "I hope it doesn't happen this year. Poor Timothy's too sick to move."

"Sick, is he? Take him to Mr Ages."

"I've been myself. But he was too weak to get out of bed, and still is."

"I'm sorry to hear that. Then we must hope for another frost, or that the tractor will break down. I wish someone would drive a tractor through his house and see how he likes it." So muttering, the lady shrew moved off, and Mrs Frisby continued across the garden. The remark was illogical, of course, for they both knew that without Mr Fitzgibbon's plough there would be no garden to live in at all, and there was no way he could turn the earth without also turning up their houses.

Or was there? What the shrew had said was meant to be sympathetic, but it was not helpful. It meant, Mrs Frisby realized, that she, too, could see no solution to the problem. But that did not mean that there was none. She remembered something her husband, Mr Frisby, used to say: All doors are hard to unlock until you have the key. All right. She must try to find the key. But where? Whom to ask?

And then, as if to make things worse, she heard a sound that filled her with alarm. It came from across the fence in the farmyard, a loud, sputtering roar. It was Farmer Fitzgibbon starting his tractor.

INTRODUCTION

No book of classic animal stories would be complete without a contribution from Dick King-Smith. This is one of his funniest, a simple idea masterfully accomplished. We are thrown into the hedgehogs' dilemma right from the very first page. "Your Auntie Betty's copped it", Pa Hedgehog says to Ma. It's not difficult to guess how Auntie Betty 'copped it'. The traffic where they live has become so dreadful that crossing the road safely is almost impossible. When young Max hears about his auntie, he is determined to find out how human beings manage to cross the road without being run over. His research leads him to a zebra crossing, and he decides to try it out for himself . . .

THE HODGEHEG

DICK KING-SMITH

By now it was quite late. The rush hour was over. The shops were shut. All was quiet. *I'll wait*, thought Max, *and then when a car or lorry comes along I'll cross in front of it.*

Soon he saw something coming. It was a lorry. He was halfway across when he suddenly realized that the lorry hadn't slowed up at all and was almost on top of him, blinding him with its brilliant lights, deafening him with its thunderous roar. It was not going to stop! Lorries only stopped for people – not hedgehogs!

The lorry driver, who, until he was almost upon the crossing, had been quite unaware of the tiny pedestrian, did the only possible thing. With no time to brake or swerve, he steered so as to straddle the little animal. Looking back in his wing-mirror,

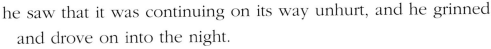

he saw that it was continuing on its way unhurt, and he grinned and drove on into the night.

The sheer horror of this great monster passing above with its huge wheels on either side of him threw Max into a blind panic, and he made for the end of the crossing as fast as his legs would carry him. He did not see the cyclist silently pedalling along close to the kerb and the cyclist did not see him until the last moment. Feverishly the man twisted his handlebars, and the front wheel of his bicycle, suddenly wrenched round, caught Max on the rump and catapulted him head first into the face of the kerbstone.

The next thing that Max recalled was crawling painfully under his own front gate. Somehow he had managed to come back over the zebra crossing. He had known nothing of the concern of the cyclist, who had dismounted, peered at what looked like a small dead hedgehog, sighed and pedalled sadly away. He remembered nothing of his journey home, wobbling dazedly along on the now deserted pavement, guided only by his sense of smell. All he knew was that he had an awful headache.

The family had crowded round him on his return, all talking at once.

"Where have you been all this time?" asked Ma.

"Are you all right, son?" asked Pa.

"Did you cross the road?" they both said, and Peony, Pansy and Petunia echoed, "Did you? Did you? Did you?"

For a while Max did not reply. His thoughts were muddled, and when he did speak, his words were muddled too.

"I got a head on the bump," he said slowly.

The family looked at one another.

"Something bot me on the hittom," said Max, "and then I headed my bang. My ache bads headly."

"But did you cross the road?" cried his sisters.

"Yes," said Max wearily. "I hound where the fumans cross over, but —"

"But the traffic only stops if you're a human?" interrupted Pa.

"Yes," said Max. "Not if you're a hodgeheg."

INTRODUCTION

The last thing Tom wants to do when his parents go away on the trip of a lifetime is to stay on Aunt Millie's farm. Animals don't like him, he says, he'll miss his friend, Petie, and he'll be expected to do things that he'll be hopeless at. He has no choice, however, and his worst fears are quickly realized when he is given his cousin's room at the farm. His cousin is clearly into all sorts of sports and country pursuits, which don't interest Tom in the slightest. For the first few days, Tom mooches around, eating little, keeping himself to himself, writing letters to his friend, until one afternoon, when he is sitting in a field by a creek, he spots a very unusual fox. That one sighting is to change everything . . .

THE MIDNIGHT FOX

BETSY BYARS

The Black Fox

The first three days on the farm were the longest, slowest days
of my life. It seemed to me in those days that nothing was
moving at all, not air, not time. Even the bees, the biggest, fattest
bees that I had ever seen, just seemed to hang in the air. The
problem, or one of them, was that I was not an enormously
adaptable person and I did not fit into new situations well.

I did a lot of just standing around those first days. I would be
standing in the kitchen and Aunt Millie would turn around, stirring
something, and bump into me and say, "Oh, my goodness! You
gave me a scare. I didn't even hear you come in. When did you
come in?"

"Just a minute ago."

"Well, I didn't hear you. You are so quiet."

Or Uncle Fred would come out of the barn wiping his hands on a rag and there I'd be, just standing, and he'd say, "Well, boy, how's it going?"

"Fine, Uncle Fred."

"Good! Good! Don't get in any mischief, now."

"I won't."

I spent a lot of time at the pond and walking down the road and back. I spent about an hour one afternoon hitting the end of an old rope swing that was hanging from a tree in the front yard. I made my two models, and then I took some of the spare plastic strips and rigged up a harness, so that the horse was pulling the car, and Aunt Millie got very excited over this bit of real nothing and said it was the cleverest thing she had ever seen.

I wrote a long letter to Petie. I went down to the stream and made boats of twigs and leaves and watched them float out of sight. I looked through about a hundred farm magazines. I weeded Aunt Millie's flowers while she stood over me saying, "Not that, not that, that's a zinnia. Get the chickweed – see? Right here." And she would snatch it up for me. I had none of the difficult chores that I had expected because the farm was so well run that everything was already planned without me. In all my life I have never spent longer, more miserable days, and I had to keep saying, "I'm fine, just fine," because people were asking how I was all the time.

The one highlight of my day was to go down to the mailbox for the mail. This was the only thing I did all day that was of any use. Then, too, the honking of the mail truck would give me the feeling that there was a letter of great importance waiting for me in the box. I could hardly hurry down the road fast enough.

Anyone watching me from behind would probably have seen only a cloud of dust, my feet would pound so fast. So far, the only mail I had received was a postcard from my mom with a picture of the Statue of Liberty on it telling me how excited and happy she was.

This Thursday morning when I went to the mailbox there was a letter to me from Petie Burkis and I was never so glad to see anything in my life. I ripped it open and completely destroyed the envelope I was in such a hurry. And I thought that when I was a hundred years old, sitting in a chair with a rug over my knees, and my mail was brought in on a silver tray, if there was a letter from Petie Burkis on that tray, I would snatch it up and rip it open just like this. I could hardly get it unfolded – Petie folds his letters up small – I was so excited.

Dear Tom,

There is nothing much happening here. I went to the playground Saturday after you left, and you know that steep bank by the swings? Well, I fell all the way down that. Here's the story:

Boy falls down bank while girl onlookers cheer

Today Petie Burkis fell down the bank at Harley Playground. It is reported that some ill-mannered girls at the park for a picnic cheered and laughed at the sight of the young, demolished boy. The brave youngster left the park unaided.

Not much else happened. Do you get Chiller Theatre? There was a real good movie on Saturday night about mushroom men.

Write me a letter,

Petie Burkis

I went in and gave the rest of the mail to Aunt Millie who said, "Well, let's see what the government's sending us today," and then I got my box of stationery and went outside.

There was a very nice place over the hill by the creek. There were trees so big I couldn't get my arms around them, and soft grass, and rocks to sit on. They were planning to let the cows into this field later on, and then it wouldn't be as nice, but now it was the best place on the farm.

Incidentally, anyone interested in butterflies would have gone crazy. There must have been a million in that one field. I had thought about there being a contest – a butterfly contest and hundreds of people would come from all over the country to catch butterflies. I had thought about it so much that I could almost see this real fat lady from Maine running all over the field with about a hundred butterfly nets and a fruit jar under her arm.

Anyway, I sat down and wrote Petie a letter.

Dear Petie,

I do not know whether we get Chiller Theatre or not. Since there is no TV set here, it is very difficult to know what we could get if we had one.

My farm chores are feeding the pigs, feeding the chickens, weeding the flowers, getting the mail, things like that. I have a lot of time to myself and I am planning a movie about a planet that collides with Earth, and this planet and Earth become fused together, and the people of Earth are terrified of the planet, because it is very weird-looking and they have heard these terrible moanlike cries coming from the depths of it. That's all so far.

Write me a letter.
Tom

I had just finished writing this letter and was waiting for a minute to see if I would think of anything to add when I looked up and saw the black fox.

I did not believe it for a minute. It was like my eyes were playing a trick or something, because I was just sort of staring across this field, thinking about my letter, and then in the distance, where the grass was very green, I saw a fox leaping over the crest of the field. The grass moved and the fox sprang towards the movement, and then, seeing that it was just the wind that had caused the grass to move, she ran straight for the grove of trees where I was sitting.

It was so great that I wanted it to start over again, like you can turn movie film back and see yourself repeat some fine thing you have done, and I wanted to see the fox leaping over the grass again. In all my life I have never been so excited.

I did not move at all, but I could hear the paper in my hand shaking, and my heart seemed to have moved up in my body and got stuck in my throat.

The fox came straight towards the grove of trees. She wasn't afraid, and I knew she had not seen me against the tree. I stayed absolutely still even though I felt like jumping up and screaming, "Aunt Millie! Uncle Fred! Come see this. It's a fox, a fox!"

Her steps as she crossed the field were lighter and quicker than a cat's. As she came closer I could see that her black fur was tipped with white. It was as if it were midnight and the moon were shining on her fur, frosting it. The wind parted her fur as it changed directions. Suddenly she stopped. She was ten feet away now, and with the changing of the wind she got my scent. She looked right at me.

I did not move for a moment and neither did she. Her head was cocked to one side, her tail curled up, her front left foot raised. In all my life I never saw anything like that fox standing there with her pale green golden eyes on me and this great black fur being blown by the wind.

Suddenly her nose quivered. It was such a slight movement I almost didn't see it, and then her mouth opened and I could see the pink tip of her tongue. She turned. She still was not afraid, but with a bound that was lighter than the wind – it was as if she was being blown away over the field – she was gone.

Still I didn't move. I couldn't. I couldn't believe that I had really seen the fox.

I had seen foxes before in zoos, but I was always in such a great hurry to get on to the good stuff that I was saying stupid things like, "I want to see the go-rilllllas," and not once had I ever really looked at a fox. Still, I could never remember seeing a black fox, not even in a zoo.

Also, there was a great deal of difference between seeing an animal in the zoo in front of painted fake rocks and trees and seeing one natural and free in the woods. It was like seeing a kite on the floor and then, later, seeing one up in the sky where it was supposed to be, pulling at the wind.

I started to pick up my pencil and write as quickly as I could, "PS Today I saw a black fox." But I didn't. This was the most exciting thing that had happened to me, and "PS Today I saw a black fox" made it nothing. "So what else is happening?" Petie Burkis would probably write back. I folded my letter, put it in an envelope, and sat there.

I thought about this old newspaper that my dad had had in his desk drawer for years. It was orange and the headline was just one word, very big, the letters about twelve inches high. WAR! And I mean it was awesome to see that word like that, because you know it was a word that was going to change your whole life, the whole world even. And every time I would see that newspaper, even though I wasn't even born when it was printed, I couldn't say anything for a minute or two.

Well, this was the way I felt right then about the black fox. I thought about a newspaper with just one word for a headline, very big, very black letters, twelve inches high. FOX! And even that did not show how awesome it had really been to me.

INTRODUCTION

*Gobbolino is a witch's kitten, but when his mother discovers
that he has blue eyes and one white paw, she knows that no
witch will employ him. And so she abandons him. As it
happens, Gobbolino has no desire to be a witch's cat, which
involves learning to ride a broomstick and turning mice into
frogs. He would rather be a kitchen cat and loved by people.*

*And so he sets off to find a new home. If only life were so
simple. One group of humans after another turns him away as
soon as he shows any signs of sorcery – which he just can't help
whenever he tries to do them a good turn. His adventures take
him to a farm, an orphanage and the Lord Mayor's mansion,
before he arrives at the window of an old man's house . . .*

GOBBOLINO
THE WITCH'S CAT
URSULA MORAY WILLIAMS

Gobbolino on Show

By evening Gobbolino came to a town. The lights in the
windows winked at him like yellow and friendly eyes:
"Come in! Come in!"

In a hundred happy homes the kettle was singing on the hob;
fat, comfortable tabbies, careless of their good fortune, dozed
under chairs, or grumbled at the noise the children made,
bouncing in from school. Fires crackled frostily, and sleepy
canaries, with dusters over their cages, twittered a last note before
tucking their downy heads under their wings.

It was the teatime hour, the hour when every cat is lord of his
house, and every house without a cat is lonely. Every cat without

a house is lonelier still, and Gobbolino trotted along missing the bright nursery fire, missing the noisy clatter of the little brothers, missing the chuckle of the baby, the clamour of the orphanage, the comfort of the farm kitchen, missing even the gloomy cavern where he had been born. He belonged to nobody, and nobody belonged to him.

He jumped on to a windowsill, peeping in through the lace curtains.

The room that he peeped into was very strange.

There was an ordinary table in the middle, certainly, and some chairs, and a kettle on the hob that sang and hissed. There were saucepans and a teapot and a blue-and-white china tea set and a clock that had lost one hand, but all the way round the room were dozens of large cages, and in each cage, sitting on a blue velvet cushion, was a cat.

A little old man stood at the table cutting up cat's-meat on twelve blue china plates.

The cats looked very happy and satisfied. Their coats were glossy, their eyes bright and intelligent, their whiskers spruce and clean.

They purred as they watched the little old man and Gobbolino heard their purring through the windowpanes.

They look very content and well cared for, thought Gobbolino. *But nobody who has so many cats already could possibly want another.*

He jumped lightly off the windowsill, but not before the little old man had seen him, for the next minute the door into the street opened wide and a voice called: "Pussy! Pussy! Pretty pussy! Come here!"

"Oh, my goodness!" said Gobbolino. "He really is calling me!"

The little old man stood at the door with a piece of cat's-meat in his hand. He picked up Gobbolino and carried him into the room where all the cages were.

"There, my pretty!" said the old man, setting him down on the table. "Oh, what a pretty cat you are! And what beautiful blue eyes you have!"

Gobbolino did not very much like being prodded and poked by the little old man's hard, bony hands. His paws were felt, his teeth examined, his whiskers counted, and his tail measured.

"Oh, what a beautiful cat you are!" the little old man said over and over again.

The other cats looked on, sitting on their velvet cushions and growling with jealousy. They had finished their cat's-meat, and all the blue china saucers were licked clean.

When he had finished poking and prodding Gobbolino, the little old man popped him into an empty cage with another blue velvet cushion in it and a saucerful of cat's-meat.

Gobbolino would have preferred to sit by the fire, but he was grateful to the little old man for taking him in, so he ate up his cat's-meat thankfully and said nothing at all.

It's nice to know there are such kind people in the world! thought Gobbolino, as he sat on his velvet cushion. *For I might have been walking all night, or have starved to death.*

"I'm sure I shall be very happy here," he said presently to his neighbour, a stately Persian madam. "But what are we all doing in these cages?"

"Don't you know?" said the Persian scornfully. "Why, you are now a show cat!"

In the morning the little old man brushed and combed the cats one by one till their fur gleamed and shone.

He was a little surprised at the coloured sparks that flew from Gobbolino's coat under the brush, but he did not stop praising him or telling him how beautiful he was.

"Such fur! Such a tail! Such colouring! And such beautiful blue eyes!" he exclaimed.

The other cats growled in their cages, for they did not like to hear the little old man praising Gobbolino.

"Ha! They're jealous!" said the little old man, and tied a red ribbon round Gobbolino's neck to make him smarter than ever.

Every morning Gobbolino was brushed and combed with the other cats, till his coat shone and gleamed as theirs did, his eyes were as bright, and his whiskers as spruce and clean.

Every morning the little old man praised and admired him from the tip of his tail to his beautiful blue eyes, while the other cats growled jealously in their cages; they would not make friends with Gobbolino.

One day the little old man was especially busy, combing his cats, brushing the velvet cushions and polishing the cages from

dark till dawn. He became very bad-tempered with his haste and exertion; scolding and hustling the cats and never once telling Gobbolino how beautiful he was.

"What is all the fuss and fluster about?" Gobbolino timidly asked his neighbour, the Persian madam.

"Don't you know?" she said scornfully. "Why, tomorrow is the Cat Show Day, and we are all going. That's what it is all about."

Gobbolino was quite excited to hear they were to have a change, for to tell the truth he had grown a little tired of his gilded cage and blue velvet cushion. He was very grateful to the little old man for giving him good food and a comfortable home, but sometimes he dreamed of a shabby rug before the fire, a cracked saucer of skim-milk, and the noisy chatter of children instead of the rows of cages, the proud unfriendly cats, the hours of brushing, and the bony hands of the little old man who poked and prodded him every morning, saying, "Oh, what a handsome little cat you are! And what beautiful blue eyes you have!"

"But I am very ungrateful!" Gobbolino told himself, sitting upright on his velvet cushion. "For I might still be wandering homeless in the cold, and here I am, well fed and cared for, sitting on a velvet cushion – Gobbolino the show cat!"

Early the next morning the little old man began to take the cages down, one by one, and pile them on to a cart drawn by a scraggy pony.

Gobbolino's cage was put on the very top of all; he had a splendid view as they trotted along the countryside towards the show.

The Cat Show was held in the Town Hall, and long before they arrived, Gobbolino could hear the excited mewing of hundreds and hundreds of show cats.

There they were, in hundreds and hundreds of cages lining the Town Hall – big cats, little cats, black cats, white cats, tabby cats, Persian cats, fat cats, thin cats, handsome cats, ugly cats, cats from China, cats from Siam, Manx cats, pet cats, wild cats, tomcats, and last of all the little old man's cats, and Gobbolino the witch's kitten with his beautiful eyes looking on at it all.

"Oh, my goodness!" he said to himself as he looked at all the cats sitting on velvet cushions of every colour under the rainbow. "Whoever will notice any of us among such splendid company?"

For the little old man had told them he expected them all to win prizes, and especially Gobbolino. He had even threatened, if they did not, to stop their cat's-meat and to take away their velvet cushions, especially Gobbolino's. He had promised to cuff all their ears, and to turn them out into the street to look after themselves as best they might, particularly Gobbolino.

The little cat's heart sank as he saw all the splendid cages and thought of the little old man's words, for nobody would look at him among such splendid company.

But the other cats sat up proud and bold. They were all certain of winning prizes, whatever Gobbolino might say.

They began to talk to their neighbours, and whispers ran from cage to cage.

"Tell me, madam, who is that black and odd-looking stranger you have brought with you? I don't think I saw him here last show."

A silky chinchilla was speaking to the Persian who had been Gobbolino's neighbour before.

"No, master adopted him lately," the Persian replied. "We don't know much about him. To tell you the truth . . ." she began to whisper and Gobbolino could not hear what she said, nor what, in her turn, the chinchilla whispered to her neighbour, till a kind of hiss was running the round of the cages, with a murmuring echo:

"Gobbolino! Gobbolino! Gobbolino!"

Gobbolino took no notice. He did not know why the cats disliked him, or why they should be jealous of him, as the little old man said they were. He felt sure they were all twenty times more handsome than himself. He wished them no harm, and if they chose to whisper about him among themselves, he did not mind.

The judges went round among the cages, looking at the cats, examining and judging.

They went away and came back again, after which the little old man gave each cat a small piece of liver, and went to sleep on a sack behind the cages.

Presently the judges brought round coloured cards and pinned them on the cats.

The Persian had a red one with "FIRST PRIZE" written on it. The chinchilla opposite had only a blue one: she was so jealous she turned her neck and would not look at the Persian till her master took her away.

Some of the other cats had coloured cards as well – red, yellow, and blue ones. The little old man trotted among his cages, well pleased, stroking the heads of his prize-winners and promising them all kinds of good things for supper.

Gobbolino was delighted to see how many prizes they would carry home in the shabby little cart. He had not even noticed that his own cage held no prize-card at all, when the chief judge stood up to announce the name of the champion – the best cat in the show.

It was Gobbolino.

For a moment there was a great silence, and then a murmuring ran through the Town Hall that rose to a hissing. It came from the cages.

The hissing grew to a spitting, and the spitting to a yowling.

In vain the judges tried to quell the noise, in vain the owners rattled on the cages or covered them with rugs – the angry cats yowled on and on, till one great voice arose from every cage announcing:

"But Gobbolino is a witch's cat!"

The judges turned pale, so did the owners.

The cat-fanciers, who had come to buy, looked at each other in horror, for each of them had been ready to offer the little old man large sums of money for Gobbolino.

The little old man himself, crimson with fury, shook his fist at the judges, and then at Gobbolino, while round and round the cages ran the angry murmur.

"Gobbolino is a witch's cat."

"Oh, my goodness!" said Gobbolino, cowering on the blue velvet cushion in a corner of his cage. "Why was I born a witch's cat, oh why? I don't want to win prizes!" he sobbed. "I don't want to be a champion and have people admire me! I only want a friendly home with kindly people, that's not very much to ask. But oh, my goodness! What is going to happen to me now?"

He was not left long in doubt, for the angry judge turned on the little old man and ordered him to leave the Town Hall immediately. His cats were all disqualified, and especially Gobbolino. The little old man was bundled out into the street with all his cages, and at the last moment the judges sent his prize-cards after him. Perhaps after all, they said, he had not known he was showing a witch's cat.

But the little old man's rage was not cooled by saving his prize-cards.

He opened the door of Gobbolino's cage and dropped him out into the road.

"Miserable creature!" he raged. "Look what trouble you have brought upon me! Why didn't you tell me you were a witch's kitten? Be off with you directly and let me never see a whisker of your face again!"

He whipped up the scraggy pony and galloped away in a cloud of dust, with the cats' cages rocketing and banging, and the cats peering and mocking over their shoulders at Gobbolino.

He was not sorry to see the last of them, or to stretch his paws, which had become very cramped and stiff from sitting so long on a velvet cushion.

He was very sorry to have brought such trouble upon the little old man, but he had never really enjoyed being a show cat, and living in a cage had become very irksome and monotonous.

I am sure there is a home not far away where I shall be welcome, thought Gobbolino.

INTRODUCTION

When the naturalist Gerald Durrell was 10, his family decided to leave the cold, windswept shores of England and begin a new life on the island of Corfu. Durrell's account of the time they spent there is hilarious, peopled with wonderful characters. He was already fascinated by wildlife, and in his memoir the young Gerald soon discovers that the garden surrounding their little villa is full of creatures he has never seen before. He spends hours exploring every nook and cranny. Some of his discoveries find their way into the villa, much to the horror of the other members of his family . . .

MY FAMILY AND OTHER ANIMALS

GERALD DURRELL

The World in a Wall

The crumbling wall that surrounded the sunken garden alongside the house was a rich hunting ground for me. It was an ancient brick wall that had been plastered over, but now this outer skin was green with moss, bulging and sagging with the damp of many winters. The whole surface was an intricate map of cracks, some several inches wide, others as fine as hairs. Here and there large pieces had dropped off and revealed the rows of rose-pink bricks lying beneath like ribs. There was a whole landscape on this wall if you peered closely enough to see it; the roofs of a hundred tiny toadstools, red, yellow and brown,

showed in patches like villages on the damper portions; mountains of bottle-green moss grew in tuffets so symmetrical that they might have been planted and trimmed; forests of small ferns sprouted from cracks in the shady places, drooping languidly like little green fountains. The top of the wall was a desert land, too dry for anything except a few rust-red mosses to live in it, too hot for anything except sunbathing by the dragonflies. At the base of the wall grew a mass of plants – cyclamen, crocus, asphodel – thrusting their leaves among the piles of broken and chipped roof-tiles that lay there. This whole strip was guarded by a labyrinth of blackberry that hung, in season, with fruit that was plump and juicy and black as ebony.

The inhabitants of the wall were a mixed lot, and they were divided into day and night workers, the hunters and the hunted. At night the hunters were the toads that lived among the brambles, and the geckos, pale, translucent, with bulging eyes, that lived in the cracks higher up the wall. Their prey was the population of stupid, absent-minded crane-flies that zoomed and banged their way among the leaves; moths of all sizes and shapes, moths striped, tessellated, checked, spotted, and blotched, that fluttered in soft clouds along the withered plaster; the beetles, rotund and neatly clad as businessmen, hurrying with portly efficiency about their night's work. When the last glow-worm had dragged his frosty emerald lantern to bed over the hills of moss, and the sun rose, the wall was taken over by the next set of inhabitants. Here it was more difficult to differentiate between the prey and the predators, for everything seemed to feed indiscriminately off everything else. Thus the hunting wasps searched out caterpillars and spiders; the spiders hunted for flies; the dragonflies, big, brittle and hunting-pink, fed off the spiders and the flies; and the swift, lithe, and multicoloured wall lizards fed off everything.

But the shyest and most self-effacing of the wall community were the most dangerous; you hardly ever saw one unless you looked for it, and yet there must have been several hundred living in the cracks of the wall. Slide a knife-blade carefully under a piece of the loose plaster and lever it gently away from the brick, and there, crouching beneath it, would be a little black scorpion an inch long, looking as though he were made out of polished chocolate. They were weird-looking little things, with their flattened, oval bodies, their neat, crooked legs, and enormous crab-like claws, bulbous and neatly jointed as armour, and the tail like a string of brown beads ending in a sting like a rose-thorn. The scorpion would lie there quite quietly as you examined him, only raising his tail in an almost apologetic gesture of warning if

you breathed too hard on him. If you kept him in the sun too long he would simply turn his back on you and walk away, and then slide slowly but firmly under another section of plaster.

I grew very fond of these scorpions. I found them to be pleasant, unassuming creatures with, on the whole, the most charming habits. Provided you did nothing silly or clumsy (like putting your hand on one) the scorpions treated you with respect, their one desire being to get away and hide as quickly as possible. They must have found me rather a trial, for I was always ripping sections of the plaster away so that I could watch them, or capturing them and making them walk about in jam jars so that I could see the way their feet moved. By means of my sudden and unexpected assaults on the wall I discovered quite a bit about the scorpions. I found that they would eat bluebottles (though how they caught them was a mystery I never solved), grasshoppers, moths, and lacewing flies. Several times I found one of them eating another, a habit I found most distressing in a creature otherwise so impeccable.

By crouching under the wall at night with a torch, I managed to catch some brief glimpses of the scorpions' wonderful courtship dances. I saw them standing, claws clasped, their bodies raised to the skies, their tails lovingly entwined; I saw them waltzing slowly in circles among the moss cushions, claw in claw. But my view of these performances was all too short, for almost as soon as I switched on the torch the partners would stop, pause for a moment, and then, seeing that I was not going to extinguish the light, would turn round and walk firmly away, claw in claw, side by side. They were definitely beasts that believed in keeping themselves to themselves. If I could have kept a colony in captivity I would probably have been able to see the whole of the courtship, but the family had forbidden scorpions in the house, despite my arguments in favour of them.

Then one day I found a fat female scorpion in the wall, wearing what at first glance appeared to be a pale fawn fur coat. Closer inspection proved that this strange garment was made up of a mass of tiny babies clinging to the mother's back. I was enraptured by this family, and I made up my mind to smuggle them into the house and up to my bedroom so that I might keep them and watch them grow up. With infinite care I manoeuvred the mother and family into a matchbox, and then hurried to the villa. It was rather unfortunate that just as I entered the door lunch should be served; however, I placed the matchbox carefully on the mantelpiece in the drawing room, so that the scorpions should get plenty of air, and made my way to the dining room and joined the family for the meal. Dawdling over my food, feeding Roger surreptitiously under the table, and listening to the family arguing, I completely forgot about my exciting new captures. At last Larry, having finished, fetched the cigarettes from the drawing room, and lying back in his chair he put one in his mouth and picked up the matchbox he had brought. Oblivious of my impending doom I watched him interestedly as, still talking glibly, he opened the matchbox.

Now I maintain to this day that the female scorpion meant no harm. She was agitated and a trifle annoyed at being shut up in a matchbox for so long, and so she seized the first opportunity to escape. She hoisted herself out of the box with great rapidity, her babies clinging on desperately, and scuttled onto the back of Larry's hand. There, not quite certain what to do next, she paused, her sting curved up at the ready. Larry, feeling the movement of her claws, glanced down to see what it was, and from that moment things got increasingly confused.

He uttered a roar of fright that made Lugaretzia drop a plate and brought Roger out from beneath the table, barking wildly.

With a flick of his hand he sent the unfortunate scorpion flying down the table, and she landed midway between Margo and Leslie, scattering babies like confetti as she thumped onto the cloth. Thoroughly enraged at this treatment, the creature sped towards Leslie, her sting quivering with emotion. Leslie leaped to his feet, overturning his chair, and flicked out desperately with his napkin, sending the scorpion rolling across the cloth towards Margo, who promptly let out a scream that any railway engine would have been proud to produce. Mother, completely bewildered by the sudden and rapid change from peace to chaos, put on her glasses and peered down the table to see what was causing the pandemonium, and at that moment Margo, in a vain attempt to stop the scorpion's advance, hurled a glass of water at it. The shower missed the animal completely, but successfully drenched Mother, who, not being able to stand cold water, promptly lost her breath and sat gasping at the end of the table, unable even to protest. The scorpion had now gone to ground under Leslie's plate, while her babies swarmed wildly all over the table. Roger, mystified by the panic, but determined to do his share, ran round and round the room, barking hysterically.

"It's that bloody boy again . . . " bellowed Larry.

"Look out! Look out! They're coming!" screamed Margo.

"All we need is a book," roared Leslie; "don't panic, hit 'em with a book."

"What on earth's the matter with you all?" Mother kept imploring, mopping her glasses.

"It's that bloody boy . . . he'll kill the lot of us . . . Look at the table . . . knee-deep in scorpions . . . "

"Quick . . . quick . . . do something . . . Look out, look out!"

"Stop screeching and get a book, for God's sake . . . You're worse than the dog . . . Shut up, Roger . . . "

"By the grace of God I wasn't bitten . . ."

"Look out . . . there's another one . . . Quick, quick, do something . . . "

"Oh, shut up and get me a book or something . . . "

"But how did the scorpions get on the table, dear?"

"That bloody boy . . . Every matchbox in the house is a death-trap . . ."

"Look out, it's coming towards me . . . Quick, quick, do something . . . "

"Hit it with your knife . . . your knife . . . Go on, hit it . . . "

Since no one had bothered to explain things to him, Roger was under the mistaken impression that the family were being attacked, and that it was his duty to defend them. As Lugaretzia was the only stranger in the room, he came to the logical

conclusion that she must be the responsible party, so he bit her in the ankle. This did not help matters very much.

By the time a certain amount of order had been restored, all the baby scorpions had hidden themselves under various plates and bits of cutlery. Eventually, after impassioned pleas on my part, backed up by Mother, Leslie's suggestion that the whole lot be slaughtered was quashed. While the family, still simmering with rage and fright, retired to the drawing room, I spent half an hour rounding up the babies, picking them up in a teaspoon, and returning them to their mother's back. Then I carried them outside on a saucer and, with the utmost reluctance, released them onto the garden wall. Roger and I went and spent the afternoon on the hillside, for I felt it would be prudent to allow the family to have a siesta before seeing them again.

INTRODUCTION

Gerald Durrell, commenting on this book, wrote, "It must surely be one of the most remarkable cases on record of a human being's association with a wild animal." First published in 1960, Born Free *is the story of a lioness – Elsa – from her earliest days, when she had to be hand-reared, until her return to the wild as a fully grown adult. Joy Adamson describes every moment of Elsa's young life and the bond that grew between them, a bond so strong that even when Elsa was capable of breaking a neck with one cuff of her giant paw, Joy and her husband George never felt themselves to be in danger.*

BORN FREE

JOY ADAMSON

It was an exciting moment when the cub met her first elephant, an anxious one too, for poor Elsa had no mother to warn her against these animals who regard lion as the only enemies of their young and therefore sometimes kill them. One day Nuru, who had taken her out for her morning walk, came back panting to say that Elsa was "playing with an elephant". We took our rifles and he guided us to the scene. There we saw a great old elephant, his head buried in a bush, enjoying his breakfast. Suddenly Elsa, who had crept up from behind, took a playful swipe at one of his hind legs. A scream of shocked surprise and injured dignity followed this piece of impertinence. Then the elephant backed from the bush and charged. Elsa hopped nimbly out of his way, and quite unimpressed began to stalk him. It was a very funny though an alarming sight, and we could only hope that we should not need to use our guns. Luckily, after a time, both became bored with the game; the old elephant went back to his meal and Elsa lay down, close by, and went to sleep.

During the next few months the cub took every opportunity that came her way to harry elephant, and there were many such occasions, for the elephant season was beginning. This meant an annual invasion by herds numbering several hundred animals. The great beasts seemed to be very familiar with the geography of Isiolo and always went to the places where the best maize and Brussels sprouts grew. Apart from this and in spite of a dense African population and motor traffic they behaved very well and gave little trouble. As our home, which is three miles distant from Isiolo, is surrounded by the best grazing, a large number of the invaders come to visit us, and an old rifle range in front of the house has become their favourite playground. At this season, we have therefore to be very careful on our walks, for small groups of elephant are always about. Now, having to protect Elsa as well as ourselves made us all the more alert.

One day at noon Nuru and Elsa returned home followed by a large number of elephant; from our dining-room window we could see them in the bush. We tried to divert her attention but she had turned and was determined to meet the advancing herd. Then, suddenly, she sat down and watched them as they turned away and walked in single file across the rifle range. It was a grand parade as one after another emerged from the bush in which Elsa crouched giving them her scent. She waited until the last of about twenty elephant had crossed, then she followed them slowly, her head held in a straight line with her shoulders, her tail outstretched.

Suddenly the big bull in the rear turned and, jerking his massive head at Elsa, screamed with a high-pitched trumpeting sound. This war cry did not intimidate her, and she walked determinedly on; so did the big elephant. We went out and, following cautiously, saw glimpses of Elsa and the elephants mingling together in the undergrowth. There were no screams nor any sound of breaking

branches, which would have indicated trouble. All the same, we waited anxiously till eventually the cub reappeared looking rather bored with the whole business.

But not all the elephants which Elsa met were so amiable as these. On another occasion she succeeded in starting a colossal stampede. The first thing we heard was tremendous thundering on the rifle range and when we reached the scene we saw a herd of elephant racing downhill, with Elsa close behind them. Finally she was charged by a single bull, but she was much too quick for him and in time he gave up the attack and followed his companions.

Giraffe provided her with great fun too. One afternoon, when we were out with her, she took on fifty. Wriggling her body close to the ground and shivering with excitement, she stalked them, advancing step by step. The giraffes took no notice of her, they just stood and watched her nonchalantly. She looked at them and then back at us, as though she wanted to say, "Why do you stand there like candlesticks and spoil my stalking?" Finally she got really cross and, rushing full speed at me, knocked me flat.

Towards sunset, we ran into a herd of elephant. The light was failing rapidly but we could just see the shapes of elephant in all directions.

It has always seemed miraculous to me that these colossal animals can move noiselessly through the bush and are thus able to surround one without warning. This time there was no doubt that we were cut off. Wherever we looked for an opening to slip through an elephant blocked the way. We tried to hold Elsa's attention, for it was not a moment for her to start one of her games with the giants. But all too soon she spotted them and dashed into their midst, then she was beyond our control. We heard screams and shrill piercing cries; my nerves were on edge, for, however carefully we manoeuvred through the dark bush, there stood an elephant confronting us. At last we managed to make our way out and reached home, but, of course, without Elsa. She only returned much later; apparently she had had great fun and certainly did not understand why I was a nervous wreck.

A euphorbia hedge borders our drive; no ordinary animal will break through it because it contains a caustic latex. If the smallest drop of this substance touches the eye it burns the membrane most painfully and will inflame it for many days. It is therefore given a wide berth by all animals except elephant, who love eating its juicy twigs and after a night's meal leave big open gaps.

Once, when I was feeding Elsa in her enclosure, I heard the unmistakeable rumbling of elephant behind this hedge which borders her wooden house and there, sure enough, were five of the giants crunching loudly and making a meal of the only barrier which stood between us. Indeed, at the time I am writing about, the hedge was already a poor sight owing to their attentions.

To add to the excitement of Elsa's life there was now a rhino living close to our house. One evening at dark, when we were returning from a walk, the cub suddenly darted behind the servants' quarters. A tremendous commotion ensued. We went to find out what it was about and saw Elsa and the rhino facing each other. After a few moments of indecision, the rhino, snorting angrily, retreated with the cub in hot pursuit.

The following evening I was walking with Elsa and Nuru, we were late and it was getting dark, when suddenly the Somali grabbed my shoulder, thus preventing me from walking straight into the rhino, which stood behind a bush, facing us. I leapt back and ran. Luckily Elsa, who had not seen the rhino, thought I was playing a game and followed me. This was fortunate, for rhinos are unpredictable creatures who are apt to charge anything, including lorries and trains. The next day, however, Elsa had her fun; she chased the animal for two miles across the valley, Nuru loyally panting after her. After this experience the rhino took itself off to quieter quarters.

By now we had established a routine for Elsa. The mornings were cool; it was then that we often watched the impala antelope leaping gracefully on the rifle range and listened to the chorus of the awakening birds. As soon as it got light Nuru released Elsa and both walked a short distance into the bush. The cub, full of unspent energy, chased everything she could find, including her own tail.

Then, when the sun got warm, she and Nuru settled under a shady tree and Elsa dozed while he read his Koran and sipped tea. Nuru always carried a rifle to protect them both against wild animals but was very good about following our instructions "to shout before shooting." He was genuinely fond of Elsa and handled her very well.

About teatime the two of them returned and we took over. First, Elsa had some milk, then we wandered into the hills or walked in the plain; she climbed trees, appeared to sharpen her claws, followed exciting scents or stalked Grant's gazelle and gerenuk, which sometimes played hide and seek with her. Much to our surprise, she was fascinated by tortoises which she rolled over and over; she loved playing, and never did she miss an opportunity of starting a game with us – we were her "pride" and she shared everything with us.

As darkness fell we returned home and took her to her enclosure, where her evening meal awaited her. It consisted of large quantities of raw meat, mostly sheep and goat; she got her roughage by breaking up the rib bones and the cartilages. As I held her bones for her I would watch the muscles on her forehead moving powerfully. I always had to scratch the marrow out for her; she licked it greedily from my fingers, resting her heavy body upright against my arms. While this went on, Pati sat on the window-sill watching us, content to know that soon her turn would come to spend the night cuddled round my neck and that then she would have me to herself.

Till then, I sat with Elsa, playing with her, sketching her or reading. These evenings were our most intimate time and I believe that her love for us was mostly fostered in these hours when, fed and happy, she could doze off with my thumb still in her mouth. It was only on moonlit nights that she became restless; then she padded along the wire, listening intently, her nostrils quivering to catch the faintest scent which might bring a message from the mysterious night outside. When she was nervous her paws became damp and I could often judge her state of mind by holding them in my hands.

INTRODUCTION

The Wind in the Willows *is my favourite children's book.*
I discovered it as a child, rediscovered it through the stage
version, Toad of Toad Hall, *have retold it for younger*
children, and live with fond memories of its wonderful
characters. And they are wonderful characters: the inquisitive,
vulnerable young Mole; the practical, kindly Rat; the wise,
avuncular Badger; and the arrogant, disreputable, yet wholly
likeable Toad. From the moment Mole surfaces one spring day,
he begins a voyage of discovery. He meets Rat, who becomes his
companion and shows him around. They bump into Toad – or
rather he nearly bumps into them in his brand new car. And
when winter comes and Rat is mostly asleep, Mole ignores all
warnings and sets off alone into the Wild Wood to visit Badger.
It's just as well Rat wakes in time to save his friend, and they
arrive on Badger's doorstep together.

THE WIND IN THE WILLOWS

KENNETH GRAHAME

Mr Badger's House

They waited patiently for what seemed a very long time, stamping in the snow to keep their feet warm. At last they heard the sound of slow shuffling footsteps approaching the door from the inside. It seemed, as the Mole remarked to the Rat, like someone walking in carpet slippers that were too large for him and down at heel; which was intelligent of Mole, because that was exactly what it was.

There was the noise of a bolt shot back, and the door opened a few inches, enough to show a long snout and a pair of sleepy, blinking eyes.

"Now, the very next time this happens," said a gruff and suspicious voice, "I shall be exceedingly angry. Who is it this time, disturbing people on such a night? Speak up!"

"Oh, Badger," cried Rat, "let us in, please. It's me, Rat, and my friend Mole, and we've lost our way in the snow."

"What, Ratty, my dear little man!" exclaimed the Badger, in quite a different voice. "Come along in, both of you, at once. Why, you must be perished. Well I never! Lost in the snow! And in the Wild Wood, too, and at this time of night! But come in with you."

The two animals tumbled over each other in their eagerness to get inside, and heard the door shut behind them with great joy and relief.

The Badger, who wore a long dressing gown, and whose slippers were indeed very down at heel, carried a flat candlestick in his paw and had probably been on his way to bed when their summons sounded. He looked kindly down on them and patted both their heads. "This is not the sort of night for small animals to be out," he said paternally. "I'm afraid you've been up to some of your pranks again, Ratty. But come along; come into the kitchen. There's a first-rate fire there, and supper and everything."

He shuffled on in front of them, carrying the light, and they followed him, nudging each other in an anticipating sort of way, down a long, gloomy, and, to tell the truth, decidedly shabby passage, into a sort of central hall, out of which they could dimly see other long tunnel-like passages branching, passages mysterious and without apparent end. But there were doors in the hall as well – stout oaken comfortable-looking doors. One of these the Badger flung open, and at once they found themselves in all the glow and warmth of a large fire-lit kitchen.

The floor was well-worn red brick, and on the wide hearth burnt a fire of logs, between two attractive chimney-corners tucked away in the wall, well out of any suspicion of draught. A couple of high-backed settles, facing each other on either side of the fire, gave further sitting accommodation for the sociably disposed. In the middle of the room stood a long table of plain boards placed on trestles, with benches down each side. At one end of it, where an armchair stood pushed back, were spread the remains of the Badger's plain but ample supper. Rows of spotless plates winked from the shelves of the dresser at the far end of the room, and from the rafters overhead hung hams, bundles of dried herbs, nets of onions, and baskets of eggs. It seemed a place where heroes could fitly feast after victory, where weary harvesters could line up in scores along the table and keep their Harvest Home with mirth and song, or where two or three friends of simple tastes could sit about as they pleased and eat and smoke and talk in comfort and contentment. The ruddy brick floor smiled up at the smoky ceiling; the oaken settles, shiny with long wear, exchanged cheerful glances with each other; plates on the dresser grinned at pots on the shelf, and the merry firelight flickered and played over everything without distinction.

The kindly Badger thrust them down on a settle to toast themselves at the fire, and bade them remove their wet coats and boots. Then he fetched them dressing gowns and slippers, and himself bathed the Mole's shin with warm water and mended the cut with sticking-plaster till the whole thing was just as good as new, if not better. In the embracing light and warmth, warm and dry at last, with weary legs propped up in front of them, and a suggestive clink of plates being arranged on the table behind, it seemed to the storm-driven animals, now in safe anchorage, that the

cold and trackless Wild Wood just left outside was miles and miles away, and all that they had suffered in it a half-forgotten dream.

When at last they were thoroughly toasted, the Badger summoned them to the table, where he had been busy laying a repast. They had felt pretty hungry before, but when they actually saw at last the supper that was spread for them, really it seemed only a question of what they should attack first where all was so attractive, and whether the other things would obligingly wait for them till they had time to give them attention. Conversation was impossible for a long time; and when it was slowly resumed, it was that regrettable sort of conversation that results from talking with your mouth full. The Badger did not mind that sort of thing at all, nor did he take any notice of elbows on the table, or everybody speaking at once. As he did not go into Society himself, he had got an idea that these things belonged to the things that didn't really matter. (We know of course that he was wrong, and took too narrow a view; because they do matter very much, though it would take too long to explain why.) He sat in his armchair at the head of the table, and nodded gravely at intervals as the animals told their story; and he did not seem surprised or shocked at anything, and he never said, "I told you so," or "Just what I always said," or remarked that they ought to have done so-and-so, or ought not to have done something else. The Mole began to feel very friendly towards him.

When supper was really finished at last, and each animal felt that his skin was now as tight as was decently safe, and that by this time he didn't care a hang for anybody or anything, they gathered round the glowing embers of the great wood fire, and thought how jolly it was to be sitting up so late, and so independent, and so full; and after they had chatted for a time about things in general, the Badger said heartily, "Now then!

Tell us the news from your part of the world. How's old Toad going on?"

"Oh, from bad to worse," said the Rat gravely, while the Mole, cocked up on a settle and basking in the firelight, his heels higher than his head, tried to look properly mournful. "Another smash-up only last week, and a bad one. You see, he will insist on driving himself, and he's hopelessly incapable. If he'd only employ a

decent, steady, well-trained animal, pay him good wages, and leave everything to him, he'd get on all right. But no; he's convinced he's a heaven-born driver, and nobody can teach him anything; and all the rest follows."

"How many has he had?" inquired the Badger gloomily.

"Smashes, or machines?" asked the Rat. "Oh, well, after all, it's the same thing – with Toad. This is the seventh. As for the others – you know that coach-house of his? Well, it's piled up – literally piled up to the roof – with fragments of motor-cars, none of them bigger than your hat! That accounts for the other six – so far as they can be accounted for."

"He's been in hospital three times," put in the Mole; "and as for the fines he's had to pay, it's simply awful to think of."

"Yes, and that's part of the trouble," continued the Rat. "Toad's rich, we all know; but he's not a millionaire. And he's a hopelessly bad driver, and quite regardless of law and order. Killed or ruined – it's got to be one of the two things, sooner or later. Badger! We're his friends – oughtn't we to do something?"

The Badger went through a bit of hard thinking. "Now look here!" he said at last, rather severely; "of course you know I can't do anything now?"

His two friends assented, quite understanding his point. No animal, according to the rules of animal-etiquette, is ever expected to do anything strenuous, or heroic, or even moderately active during the off-season of winter. All are sleepy – some actually asleep. All are weather-bound, more or less; and all are resting from arduous days and nights, during which every muscle in them has been severely tested, and every energy kept at full stretch.

"Very well then!" continued the Badger. "But, when once the year has really turned, and the nights are shorter, and halfway through them one rouses and feels fidgety and wanting to be up

and doing by sunrise, if not before – you know! – ”

Both animals nodded gravely. They knew!

“Well, then,” went on the Badger, “we – that is, you and me and
our friend the Mole here – we'll take Toad seriously in hand. We'll
stand no nonsense whatever. We'll bring him back to reason, by
force if need be. We'll make him be a sensible Toad. We'll – you're
asleep, Rat!”

“Not me!” said the Rat, waking up with a jerk.

“He's been asleep two or three times since supper,” said the
Mole, laughing. He himself was feeling quite wakeful and even
lively, though he didn't know why. The reason was, of course, that

he being naturally an underground animal by birth and breeding, the situation of Badger's house exactly suited him and made him feel at home; while the Rat, who slept every night in a bedroom the windows of which opened on a breezy river, naturally felt the atmosphere still and oppressive.

"Well, it's time we were all in bed," said the Badger, getting up and fetching flat candlesticks. "Come along, you two, and I'll show you your quarters. And take your time tomorrow morning – breakfast at any hour you please!"

He conducted the two animals to a long room that seemed half bedchamber and half loft. The Badger's winter stores, which indeed were visible everywhere, took up half the room – piles of apples, turnips and potatoes, baskets full of nuts, and jars of honey; but the two little white beds on the remainder of the floor looked soft and inviting, and the linen on them, though coarse, was clean and smelt beautifully of lavender; and the Mole and the Water Rat, shaking off their garments in some thirty seconds, tumbled in between the sheets in great joy and contentment.

In accordance with the kindly Badger's injunctions, the two tired animals came down to breakfast very late next morning, and found a bright fire burning in the kitchen, and two young hedgehogs sitting on a bench at the table, eating oatmeal porridge out of wooden bowls. The hedgehogs dropped their spoons, rose to their feet, and ducked their heads respectfully as the two entered.

"There, sit down, sit down," said the Rat pleasantly, "and go on with your porridge. Where have you youngsters come from? Lost your way in the snow, I suppose?"

"Yes please, sir," said the elder of the two hedgehogs respectfully. "Me and little Billy here, we was trying to find our way to school – Mother would have us go, was the weather ever so – and of course we lost ourselves, sir, and Billy he got

frightened and took and cried, being young and faint-hearted. And at last we happened up against Mr Badger's back door, and made so bold as to knock, sir, for Mr Badger he's a kind-hearted gentleman, as everyone knows – "

"I understand," said the Rat, cutting himself some rashers from a side of bacon, while the Mole dropped some eggs into a saucepan. "And what's the weather like outside? You needn't 'sir' me quite so much," he added.

"O, terrible bad, sir, terrible deep the snow is," said the hedgehog. "No getting out for the likes of you gentlemen today."

"Where's Mr Badger?" inquired the Mole, as he warmed the coffee-pot before the fire.

"The master's gone into his study, sir," replied the hedgehog, "and he said as how he was going to be particular busy this morning, and on no account was he to be disturbed."

This explanation, of course, was thoroughly understood by every one present. The fact is, as already set forth, when you live a life of intense activity for six months in the year, and of comparative or actual somnolence for the other six, during the latter period you cannot be continually pleading sleepiness when there are people about or things to be done. The excuse gets monotonous. The animals well knew that Badger, having eaten a hearty breakfast, had retired to his study and settled himself in an armchair with his legs up on another and a red cotton handkerchief over his face, and was being "busy" in the usual way at this time of the year.

The front-door bell clanged loudly, and the Rat, who was very greasy with buttered toast, sent Billy, the smaller hedgehog, to see who it might be. There was a sound of much stamping in the hall, and presently Billy returned in front of the Otter, who threw himself on the Rat with an embrace and a shout of affectionate greeting.

"Get off!" spluttered the Rat, with his mouth full.

"Thought I should find you here all right," said the Otter cheerfully. "They were all in a great state of alarm along River Bank when I arrived this morning. Rat never been home all night – nor Mole either – something dreadful must have happened, they said; and the snow had covered up all your tracks, of course. But I knew that when people were in any fix they mostly went to Badger, or else Badger got to know of it somehow, so I came straight off here, through the Wild Wood and the snow! My! It was fine, coming through the snow as the red sun was rising and showing against the black tree trunks! As you went along in

the stillness, every now and then masses of snow slid off the branches suddenly with a flop! Making you jump and run for cover. Snow-castles and snow-caverns had sprung up out of nowhere in the night – and snow-bridges, terraces, ramparts – I could have stayed and played with them for hours. Here and there great branches had been torn away by the sheer weight of the snow, and robins perched and hopped on them in their perky conceited way, just as if they had done it themselves. A ragged string of wild geese passed overhead, high on the grey sky, and a few rooks whirled over the trees, inspected, and flapped off homewards with a disgusted expression; but I met no sensible being to ask the news of. About halfway across I came on a rabbit

sitting on a stump, cleaning his silly face with his paws. He was a pretty scared animal when I crept up behind him and placed a heavy forepaw on his shoulder. I had to cuff his head once or twice to get any sense out of it at all. At last I managed to extract from him that Mole had been seen in the Wild Wood last night by one of them. It was the talk of the burrows, he said, how Mole, Mr Rat's particular friend, was in a bad fix; how he had lost his way, and 'They' were up and out hunting, and were chivvying him round and round. 'Then why didn't any of you do something?' I asked. 'You mayn't be blest with brains, but there are hundreds and hundreds of you, big, stout fellows, as fat as butter and your burrows running in all directions, and you could have taken him in, and made him safe and comfortable, or tried to, at all events.' 'What, us?' he merely said: 'do something? Us rabbits?' So I cuffed him again and left him. There was nothing else to be done. At any rate, I had learnt something; and if I had had the luck to meet any of 'Them' I'd have learnt something more – or they would."

"Weren't you at all – er – nervous?" asked the Mole, some of yesterday's terror coming back to him at the mention of the Wild Wood.

"Nervous?" The Otter showed a gleaming set of strong white teeth as he laughed. "I'd give 'em nerves if any of them tried anything on with me. Here, Mole, fry me some slices of ham, like the good little chap you are. I'm frightfully hungry, and I've got any amount to say to Ratty here. Haven't seen him for an age."

So the good-natured Mole, having cut some slices of ham, set the hedgehogs to fry it, and returned to his own breakfast, while the Otter and the Rat, their heads together, eagerly talked river-shop, which is long shop and talk that is endless, running on like the babbling river itself.

INTRODUCTION

We are taken back to a different era in this wonderfully
evocative book — an era where at mealtimes children are not
supposed to speak, and where a schoolteacher disciplines
unruly pupils with a blacksnake ox-whip! Much of the story
is about nine-year-old Almanzo, and how he learns all the
skills of a farmer — like breaking calves, milking cows and
grooming horses — on his family's farm in upstate New York.
It is not until he has gained his father's trust that he is
allowed to have his very own horse.

FARMER BOY

LAURA INGALLS WILDER

Sheep Shearing

Now the meadows and pastures were velvety with thick grass, and the weather was warm. It was time to shear sheep.

On a sunny morning Pierre and Louis went with Almanzo into the pasture and they drove the sheep down to the washing-pens. The long pen ran from the grassy pasture into the clear, deep water of the Trout River. It had two gates opening into the pasture, and between the gates a short fence ran to the water's edge.

Pierre and Louis kept the flock from running away, while Almanzo took hold of a woolly sheep and pushed it through one gate. In the pen Father and Lazy John caught hold of it.

Then Almanzo pushed another one through, and Royal and French Joe caught it. The other sheep stared and bleated, and the two sheep struggled and kicked and yelled. But the men rubbed their wool full of brown soft-soap and dragged them into the deep water.

There the sheep had to swim. The men stood waist-deep in the swift water, and held on to the sheep and scrubbed them well. All the dirt came out of their wool and floated downstream with the soap suds.

When the other sheep saw this, every one of them cried, "Baa-aa-aa, baa-aa-aa!" and they all tried to run away. But Almanzo and Pierre and Louis ran yelling around the flock, and brought it back again to the gate.

As soon as a sheep was clean, the men made it swim around to the end of the dividing fence, and they boosted it up the bank into the outer side of the pen. The poor sheep came out bleating and dripping wet, but the sun soon dried it fluffy and white.

As fast as the men let go of one sheep, Almanzo pushed another into the pen, and they caught it and soaped it and dragged it into the river.

Washing sheep was fun for everybody but the sheep. The men splashed and shouted and laughed in the water, and the boys ran and shouted in the pasture. The sun was warm on their backs and the grass was cool under bare feet, and all their laughter was small in the wide, pleasant stillness of the green fields and meadows.

One sheep butted John; he sat down in the river and the water went over his head. Joe shouted, "Now if you had soap in your wool, John, you'd be ready for shearing!"

When evening came, all the sheep were washed. Clean and fluffy-white, they scattered up the slope, nibbling the grass, and the pasture looked like a snowball bush in bloom.

Next morning John came before breakfast, and Father hurried Almanzo from the table. He took a wedge of apple pie and went out to the pasture, smelling the clover and eating the spicy apples and flaky crust in big mouthfuls. He licked his fingers, and then he rounded up the sheep and drove them across the dewy grass, into the sheepfold in the South Barn.

Father had cleaned the sheepfold and built a platform across one end of it. He and Lazy John each caught a sheep, set it up on the platform, and began cutting off its wool with long shears. The thick white mat of wool peeled back, all in one piece, and the sheep was left in bare pink skin.

With the last snick of the shears the whole fleece fell on the platform, and the naked sheep jumped off it, yelling, "Baa-aa-aa!" All the other sheep yelled back at the sight, but already Father and John were shearing two more.

Royal rolled the fleece tightly and tied it with twine, and Almanzo carried it upstairs and laid it on the loft floor. He ran upstairs and down again as fast as he could, but another fleece was always ready for him.

Father and Lazy John were good sheep-shearers. Their long shears snipped through the thick wool like lightning; they cut close to the sheep, but never cut its pink skin. This was a hard thing to do, because Father's sheep were prize Merinos. Merinos have the finest wool, but their skin lies in deep wrinkles, and it is hard to get all the wool without cutting them.

Almanzo was working fast, running upstairs with the fleeces. They were so heavy that he could carry only one at a time. He didn't mean to idle, but when he saw the tabby barn-cat hurrying past with a mouse, he knew she was taking it to her new kittens.

He ran after her, and far up under the eaves of the Big Barn he found the little nest in the hay, with four kittens in it.

The tabby cat curled herself around them, loudly purring, and the black slits in her eyes widened and narrowed and widened again. The kittens' tiny pink mouths uttered tiny meows, their naked little paws had wee white claws, and their eyes were shut.

When Almanzo came back to the sheepfold, six fleeces were waiting, and Father spoke to him sternly.

"Son," he said, "see to it you keep up with us after this."

"Yes, Father," Almanzo answered, hurrying. But he heard Lazy John say:

"He can't do it. We'll be through before he is."

Then Father laughed and said:

"That's so, John. He can't keep up with us."

Almanzo made up his mind that he'd show them. If he hurried fast enough, he could keep up. Before noon he had caught up with Royal, and had to wait while a fleece was tied. So he said:

"You see, I can keep up with you!"

"Oh no, you can't!" said John. "We'll beat you. We'll be through before you are. Wait and see."

Then they all laughed at Almanzo.

They were laughing when they heard the dinner horn. Father and John finished the sheep they were shearing, and went to the house. Royal tied the last fleece and left it, and Almanzo still had to carry it upstairs. Now he understood what they meant. But he thought: *I won't let them beat me.*

He found a short rope and tied it around the neck of a sheep that wasn't sheared. He led the sheep to the stairs, and then step by step he tugged and boosted her upward. She bleated all the way, but he got her into the loft. He tied her near the fleeces and gave her some hay to keep her quiet. Then he went to dinner.

All that afternoon Lazy John and Royal kept telling him to hurry or they'd beat him. Almanzo answered:

"No, you won't. I can keep up with you."

Then they laughed at him.

He snatched up every fleece as soon as Royal tied it, and hurried upstairs and ran down again. They laughed to see him hurrying and they kept saying:

"Oh no, you won't beat us! We'll be through first."

Just before chore-time, Father and John raced to shear the last two sheep. Father beat. Almanzo ran with the fleece, and was back before the last one was tied. Royal tied it, and then he said:

"We're all through! Almanzo, we beat you! We beat you!" Royal and John burst into a great roar of laughter, and even Father laughed.

Then Almanzo said:

"No, you haven't beat me. I've got a fleece upstairs that you haven't sheared yet."

They stopped laughing, surprised. At that very minute the sheep in the loft, hearing all the other sheep let out to pasture, cried, "Baa-aa-aa!"

Almanzo shouted, "There's the fleece! I've got it upstairs and you haven't sheared it! I beat you! I beat you!"

John and Royal looked so funny that he couldn't stop laughing. Father roared with laughter.

"The joke's on you, John!" Father shouted.

INTRODUCTION

This is such a beautiful, sad story, and one I remember well from my own childhood. It's one of a collection of morality tales for children and adults by the great writer and well-known wit Oscar Wilde. At its heart are themes of social injustice, lost innocence and the redemptive power of love. First published in 1888, it still retains its power to enchant. Follow the flight of a swallow who, off to join his friends in a far-off land, settles for the night at the foot of the golden statue of a young prince.

THE HAPPY PRINCE

OSCAR WILDE

High above the city, on a tall column, stood the statue of the Happy Prince. He was gilded all over with thin leaves of fine gold, for eyes he had two bright sapphires, and a large red ruby glowed on his sword-hilt.

He was very much admired indeed. "He is as beautiful as a weathercock," remarked one of the Town Councillors who wished to gain a reputation for having artistic tastes; "only not quite so useful," he added, fearing lest people should think him unpractical, which he really was not.

"Why can't you be like the Happy Prince?" asked a sensible

mother of her little boy who was crying for the moon. "The Happy Prince never dreams of crying for anything."

"I am glad there is some one in the world who is quite happy," muttered a disappointed man as he gazed at the wonderful statue.

"He looks just like an angel," said the Charity Children as they came out of the cathedral in their bright scarlet cloaks and their clean white pinafores.

"How do you know?" said the Mathematical Master, "you have never seen one."

"Ah! but we have, in our dreams," answered the children; and the Mathematical Master frowned and looked very severe, for he did not approve of children dreaming.

One night there flew over the city a little Swallow. His friends had gone away to Egypt six weeks before, but he had stayed behind, for he was in love with the most beautiful Reed. He had met her early in the spring as he was flying down the river after a big yellow moth, and had been so attracted by her slender waist that he had stopped to talk to her.

"Shall I love you?" said the Swallow, who liked to come to the point at once, and the Reed made him a low bow. So he flew round and round her, touching the water with his wings, and making silver ripples. This was his courtship, and it lasted all through the summer.

"It is a ridiculous attachment," twittered the other Swallows; "she has no money, and far too many relations"; and indeed the river was quite full of Reeds. Then, when the autumn came they all flew away.

After they had gone he felt lonely, and began to tire of his lady-love. "She has no conversation," he said, "and I am afraid that she is a coquette, for she is always flirting with the wind." And certainly, whenever the wind blew, the Reed made the most graceful curtseys. "I admit that she is domestic," he continued, "but I love travelling, and my wife, consequently, should love travelling also."

"Will you come away with me?" he said finally to her; but the Reed shook her head, she was so attached to her home.

"You have been trifling with me," he cried. "I am off to the Pyramids. Goodbye!" and he flew away.

All day long he flew, and at night-time he arrived at the city. "Where shall I put up?" he said; "I hope the town has made preparations."

Then he saw the statue on the tall column.

"I will put up there," he cried; "it is a fine position, with plenty of fresh air." So he alighted just between the feet of the Happy Prince.

"I have a golden bedroom," he said softly to himself as he looked round, and he prepared to go to sleep; but just as he was putting his head under his wing a large drop of water fell on him.

"What a curious thing!" he cried; "there is not a single cloud in the sky, the stars are quite clear and bright, and yet it is raining. The climate in the north of Europe is really dreadful. The Reed used to like the rain, but that was merely her selfishness."

Then another drop fell.

"What is the use of a statue if it cannot keep the rain off?" he said; "I must look for a good chimney-pot," and he determined to fly away.

But before he had opened his wings, a third drop fell, and he looked up, and saw – Ah! what did he see?

The eyes of the Happy Prince were filled with tears, and tears were running down his golden cheeks. His face was so beautiful

in the moonlight that the little Swallow was filled with pity.

"Who are you?" he said.

"I am the Happy Prince."

"Why are you weeping then?" asked the Swallow; "you have quite drenched me."

"When I was alive and had a human heart," answered the statue, "I did not know what tears were, for I lived in the Palace of Sans-Souci, where sorrow is not allowed to enter. In the daytime I played with my companions in the garden, and in the evening I led the dance in the Great Hall. Round the garden ran a very lofty wall, but I never cared to ask what lay beyond it, everything about me was so beautiful. My courtiers called me the Happy Prince, and happy indeed I was, if pleasure be happiness. So I lived, and so I died. And now that I am dead they have set me up here so high that I can see all the ugliness and all the misery of my city, and though my heart is made of lead yet I cannot choose but weep."

"What! is he not solid gold?" said the Swallow to himself. He was too polite to make any personal remarks out loud.

"Far away," continued the statue in a low musical voice, "far away in a little street there is a poor house. One of the windows is open, and through it I can see a woman seated at a table. Her face is thin and worn, and she has coarse, red hands, all pricked by the needle, for she is a seamstress. She is embroidering passion-flowers on a satin gown for the loveliest of the Queen's maids-of-honour to wear at the next Court-ball. In a bed in the corner of the room her little boy is lying ill. He has a fever, and is asking for oranges. His mother has nothing to give him but river water, so he is crying. Swallow, Swallow, little Swallow, will you not bring her the ruby out of my sword-hilt? My feet are fastened to this pedestal and I cannot move."

"I am waited for in Egypt," said the Swallow. "My friends are flying up and down the Nile, and talking to the large lotus-flowers. Soon they will go to sleep in the tomb of the great King. The King is there himself in his painted coffin. He is wrapped in yellow linen, and embalmed with spices. Round his neck is a chain of pale green jade, and his hands are like withered leaves."

"Swallow, Swallow, little Swallow," said the Prince, "will you not stay with me for one night, and be my messenger? The boy is so thirsty, and the mother so sad."

"I don't think I like boys," answered the Swallow. "Last summer, when I was staying on the river, there were two rude boys, the miller's sons, who were always throwing stones at me. They never hit me, of course; we swallows fly far too well for that, and besides, I come of a family famous for its agility; but still, it was a mark of disrespect."

But the Happy Prince looked so sad that the little Swallow was sorry. "It is very cold here," he said; "but I will stay with you for one night, and be your messenger."

"Thank you, little Swallow," said the Prince.

So the Swallow picked out the great ruby from the Prince's sword, and flew away with it in his beak over the roofs of the town.

He passed by the cathedral tower, where the white marble angels were sculptured. He passed by the palace and heard the sound of dancing. A beautiful girl came out on the balcony with her lover. "How wonderful the stars are," he said to her, "and how wonderful is the power of love!"

"I hope my dress will be ready in time for the State-ball," she answered; "I have ordered passion-flowers to be embroidered on it; but the seamstresses are so lazy."

He passed over the river, and saw the lanterns hanging to the masts of the ships. He passed over the Ghetto, and saw the old

Jews bargaining with each other, and weighing out money in copper scales. At last he came to the poor house and looked in. The boy was tossing feverishly on his bed, and the mother had fallen asleep, she was so tired. In he hopped, and laid the great ruby on the table beside the woman's thimble. Then he flew gently round the bed, fanning the boy's forehead with his wings. "How cool I feel," said the boy, "I must be getting better"; and he sank into a delicious slumber.

Then the Swallow flew back to the Happy Prince, and told him what he had done. "It is curious," he remarked, "but I feel quite warm now, although it is so cold."

"That is because you have done a good action," said the Prince. And the little Swallow began to think, and then he fell asleep. Thinking always made him sleepy.

When day broke he flew down to the river and had a bath. "What a remarkable phenomenon," said the Professor of Ornithology as he was passing over the bridge. "A swallow in winter!" And he wrote a long letter about it to the local newspaper. Everyone quoted it, it was full of so many words that they could not understand.

"Tonight I go to Egypt," said the Swallow, and he was in high spirits at the prospect. He visited all the public monuments, and sat a long time on top of the church steeple. Wherever he went the Sparrows chirruped, and said to each other, "What a distinguished stranger!" so he enjoyed himself very much.

When the moon rose he flew back to the Happy Prince. "Have you any commissions for Egypt?" he cried; "I am just starting."

"Swallow, Swallow, little Swallow," said the Prince, "will you not stay with me one night longer?"

"I am waited for in Egypt," answered the Swallow. "Tomorrow my friends will fly up to the Second Cataract. The river-horse couches there among the bulrushes, and on a great granite throne sits the God Memnon. All night long he watches the stars, and when the morning star shines he utters one cry of joy, and then he is silent. At noon the yellow lions come down to the waters edge to drink. They have eyes like green beryls, and their roar is louder than the roar of the cataract."

"Swallow, Swallow, little Swallow," said the Prince, "far away across the city I see a young man in a garret. He is leaning over a desk covered with papers, and in a tumbler by his side there is a bunch of withered violets. His hair is brown and crisp, and his lips are red as a pomegranate, and he has large and dreamy eyes. He is trying to finish a play for the Director of the Theatre, but he is too cold to write any more. There is no fire in the grate, and hunger has made him faint."

"I will wait with you one night longer," said the Swallow, who really had a good heart. "Shall I take him another ruby?"

"Alas! I have no ruby now," said the Prince; "my eyes are all that I have left. They are made of rare sapphires, which were brought out of India a thousand years ago. Pluck out one of them and take it to him. He will sell it to the jeweller, and buy food and firewood, and finish his play."

"Dear Prince," said the Swallow, "I cannot do that"; and he began to weep.

"Swallow, Swallow, little Swallow," said the Prince, "do as I command you."

So the Swallow plucked out the Prince's eye, and flew away to the student's garret. It was easy enough to get in, as there was a hole in the roof. Through this he darted, and came into the room. The young man had his head buried in his hands, so he did not hear the flutter of the bird's wings, and when he looked up he found the beautiful sapphire lying on the withered violets.

"I am beginning to be appreciated," he cried; "this is from some great admirer. Now I can finish my play," and he looked quite happy.

The next day the Swallow flew down to the harbour. He sat on the mast of a large vessel and watched the sailors hauling big chests out of the hold with ropes. "Heave a-hoy!" they shouted as each chest came up. "I am going to Egypt!" cried the Swallow, but nobody minded, and when the moon rose he flew back to the Happy Prince.

"I am come to bid you goodbye," he cried.

"Swallow, Swallow, little Swallow," said the Prince, "will you not stay with me one night longer?"

"It is winter," answered the Swallow, "and the chill snow will soon be here. In Egypt the sun is warm on the green palm-trees, and the crocodiles lie in the mud and look lazily about them. My companions are building a nest in the Temple of Baalbec, and the pink and white doves are watching them, and cooing to each other. Dear Prince, I must leave you, but I will never forget you, and next spring I will bring you back two beautiful jewels in place of those you have given away. The ruby shall be redder than a red rose, and the sapphire shall be as blue as the great sea."

"In the square below," said the Happy Prince, "there stands a little match-girl. She has let her matches fall in the gutter, and they are all spoiled. Her father will beat her if she does not bring home some money, and she is crying. She has no shoes or stockings, and her little head is bare. Pluck out my other eye, and give it to her, and her father will not beat her."

"I will stay with you one night longer," said the Swallow, "but I cannot pluck out your eye. You would be quite blind then."

"Swallow, Swallow, little Swallow," said the Prince, "do as I command you."

So he plucked out the Prince's other eye, and darted down with it.

He swooped past the match-girl, and slipped the jewel into the palm of her hand. "What a lovely bit of glass," cried the little girl; and she ran home, laughing.

Then the Swallow came back to the Prince. "You are blind now," he said, "so I will stay with you always."

"No, little Swallow," said the poor Prince, "you must go away to Egypt."

"I will stay with you always," said the Swallow, and he slept at the Prince's feet.

All the next day he sat on the Prince's shoulder, and told him stories of what he had seen in strange lands. He told him of the red ibises, who stand in long rows on the banks of the Nile, and catch gold-fish in their beaks; of the Sphinx, who is as old as the world

itself, and lives in the desert, and knows everything; of the merchants, who walk slowly by the side of their camels, and carry amber beads in their hands; of the King of the Mountains of the Moon, who is as black as ebony, and worships a large crystal; of the great green snake that sleeps in a palm-tree, and has twenty priests to feed it with honey-cakes; and of the pygmies who sail over a big lake on large flat leaves, and are always at war with the butterflies.

"Dear little Swallow," said the Prince, "you tell me of marvellous things, but more marvellous than anything is the suffering of men and of women. There is no Mystery so great as Misery. Fly over my city, little Swallow, and tell me what you see there."

So the Swallow flew over the great city, and saw the rich making merry in their beautiful houses, while the beggars were sitting at the gates. He flew into dark lanes, and saw the white faces of starving children looking out listlessly at the black streets. Under the archway of a bridge two little boys were lying in one another's arms to try and keep themselves warm. "How hungry we are!" they said. "You must not lie here," shouted the Watchman, and they wandered out into the rain.

Then he flew back and told the Prince what he had seen.

"I am covered with fine gold," said the Prince, "you must take it off, leaf by leaf, and give it to my poor; the living always think that gold can make them happy."

Leaf after leaf of the fine gold the Swallow picked off, till the Happy Prince looked quite dull and grey. Leaf after leaf of the fine gold he brought to the poor, and the children's faces grew rosier, and they laughed and played games in the street. "We have bread now!" they cried.

Then the snow came, and after the snow came the frost. The streets looked as if they were made of silver, they were so bright and glistening; long icicles like crystal daggers hung down from the eaves of the houses, everybody went about in furs, and the little boys wore scarlet caps and skated on the ice.

The poor little Swallow grew colder and colder, but he would not leave the Prince, he loved him too well. He picked up crumbs outside the baker's door when the baker was not looking and tried to keep himself warm by flapping his wings.

But at last he knew that he was going to die. He had just strength to fly up to the Prince's shoulder once more. "Goodbye, dear Prince!" he murmured, "will you let me kiss your hand?"

"I am glad that you are going to Egypt at last, little Swallow," said the Prince, "you have stayed too long here; but you must kiss me on the lips, for I love you."

"It is not to Egypt that I am going," said the Swallow. "I am going to the House of Death. Death is the brother of Sleep, is he not?"

And he kissed the Happy Prince on the lips, and fell down dead at his feet.

At that moment a curious crack sounded inside the statue, as if something had broken. The fact is that the leaden heart had snapped right in two. It certainly was a dreadfully hard frost.

Early the next morning the Mayor was walking in the square below in company with the Town Councillors. As they passed the column he looked up at the statue. "Dear me! how shabby the Happy Prince looks!" he said.

"How shabby indeed!" cried the Town Councillors, who always agreed with the Mayor; and they went up to look at it.

"The ruby has fallen out of his sword, his eyes are gone, and he is golden no longer," said the Mayor, "in fact, he is little better than a beggar!"

"Little better than a beggar," said the Town Councillors.

"And here is actually a dead bird at his feet!" continued the Mayor. "We must really issue a proclamation that birds are not to be allowed

to die here." And the Town Clerk made a note of the suggestion.

So they pulled down the statue of the Happy Prince. "As he is no longer beautiful he is no longer useful," said the Art Professor at the University.

Then they melted the statue in a furnace, and the Mayor held a meeting of the Corporation to decide what was to be done with the metal. "We must have another statue, of course," he said, "and it shall be a statue of myself."

"Of myself," said each of the Town Councillors, and they quarrelled. When I last heard of them they were quarrelling still.

"What a strange thing!" said the overseer of the workmen at the foundry. "This broken lead heart will not melt in the furnace. We must throw it away." So they threw it on a dust-heap where the dead Swallow was also lying.

"Bring me the two most precious things in the city," said God to one of His Angels; and the Angel brought Him the leaden heart and the dead bird.

"You have rightly chosen," said God, "for in my garden of Paradise this little bird shall sing for evermore, and in my city of gold the Happy Prince shall praise me."

INTRODUCTION

*When their beloved owners go abroad on a temporary
assignment, Luath, a young labrador, Tao, a Siamese cat, and
Bodger, an old bull terrier, are sent to stay with a family friend.
Though the animals are not unhappy with him and he treats
them well, Luath never settles. One day, the three animals seize
the opportunity to leave, and they begin a journey which will
take them across a vast area of wooded wilderness to find their
way back home. On the way, they face great dangers and
hardship, including an encounter with a bear and its cub,
which leaves Bodger – who is already suffering from exhaustion
and lack of food – close to death. He is saved only by Tao's skill
as a hunter and Luath's tender care. Walt Disney turned the
friends' incredible journey into a film called* Homeward Bound.

THE
INCREDIBLE
JOURNEY

SHEILA BURNFORD

They slept in the same place that night and most of the
following day, and the weather mercifully continued warm and
sunny. By the third day the old dog seemed almost recovered and
the wounds were closed. He had spent most of the day ambling
around and sleeping, so that by now he seemed almost frisky and
quite eager to walk a little.

So, in the late afternoon, they left the place which had been
their home for three days and trotted slowly along the track

together again. By the time the moon rose they had travelled several miles, and they had come to the edge of a small lake which the track skirted.

A moose was standing in the water among the lily pads on the far shore, his great antlered head and humped neck silhouetted clearly against the pale moon. He took no notice of the strange animals across the water but thrust his head again and again under the surface, raising it high in the air after each immersion, and arching his neck. Two or three water hens swam out from the reeds, a little crested grebe popped up like a jack-in-the-box in the water beside them, and the spreading ripples of their wake caught the light of the moon. As the three sat, ears pricked, they watched

the moose squelch slowly out of the muddy water, shake himself, and turn cantering up the bank out of sight.

The young dog turned his head suddenly, his nose twitching, for his keen nose had caught a distant whiff of wood smoke, and of something else – something unidentifiable . . . Seconds later, the old dog caught the scent too, and started to his feet, snuffing and questioning with his nose. His thin whippy tail began to sweep to and fro and a bright gleam appeared in the slanted blackcurrant eyes. Somewhere, not too far away, were human beings – his world; he could not mistake their message – or refuse their invitation: they were undoubtedly cooking something. He trotted off determinedly in the direction of the tantalizing smell. The young dog followed somewhat reluctantly, and for once the cat passed them both; a little moon-mad perhaps, for he lay in wait to dart and strike, then streaked back into the shadows, only to reappear a second later in an elaborate stalk of their tails. Both dogs ignored him.

The scent on the evening breeze was a fragrant compound of roasting rice, wild-duck stew and wood smoke. When the animals looked down from a hill, tantalized and hungry, they saw six or seven fires in the clearing below, their flames lighting up a semicircle of tents and conical birch-bark shelters against a dark background of trees; flickering over the canoes drawn up on the edge of a wild rice marsh and dying redly in the black waters beyond; and throwing into ruddy relief the high, flat planes of brown Ojibway faces gathered around the centres of warmth and brightness.

The men were a colourful lot in jeans and bright plaid shirts, but the women were dressed in sombre colours. Two young boys, the only children there, were going from fire to fire shaking grain in shallow pans and stirring it with paddles as it parched. One man in long soft moccasins stood in a shallow pit trampling husks, half his weight supported on a log frame. Some of the band lay back from the fires, smoking and watching idly, talking softly among themselves; while others still ate, ladling the fragrant contents of a black iron pot on to tin plates. Every now and then one of them would throw a bone back over a shoulder into the bush, and the watching animals gazed hungrily after. A woman stood at the edge of the clearing pouring grain from one bark platter to another, and the loose chaff drifted off on the slight wind like smoke.

The old dog saw nothing of this, but his ears and nose supplied all that he needed to know: he could contain himself no longer and picked his way carefully down the hillside, for his shoulder still pained him. Halfway down he sneezed violently in an eddy of chaff. One of the boys by the fire looked up at the sound, his hand closing on a stone, but the woman nearby spoke sharply, and he waited, watching intently.

The old dog limped out of the shadows and into the ring of firelight, confident, friendly, and sure of his welcome; his tail wagging his whole stern ingratiatingly, ears and lips laid back in his nightmarish grimace. There was a stunned silence – broken by a wail of terror from the smaller boy, who flung himself at his mother – and then a quick excited chatter from the Indians. The old dog was rather offended and uncertain for a moment, but he made hopefully for the nearest boy, who retreated, nervously clutching his stone. But again the woman rebuked her son, and at the sharpness of her tone the old dog stopped, crestfallen. She laid down her basket then, and walked quickly across the ring of firelight, stooping down to look more closely. She spoke some soft words of reassurance, then patted his head gently and smiled at him.

The old dog leaned against her and whipped his tail against her black stockings, happy to be in contact with a human being again. She crouched down beside him to run her fingers lightly over his ears and back, and when he licked her face appreciatively, she laughed. At this, the two little boys drew nearer to the dog and the rest of the band gathered around. Soon the old dog was where he most loved to be – the centre of attention among some human beings. He made the most of it and played to an appreciative audience; when one of the men tossed him a chunk of meat he sat up painfully on his hindquarters and begged for more, waving one paw in the air. This sent the Indians into paroxysms of laughter, and he had to repeat his performance time and time again, until he was tired and lay down, panting but happy.

The Indian woman stroked him gently in reward, then ladled some of the meat from the pot out on to the grass. The old dog limped towards it; but before he ate he looked up in the direction of the hillside where he had left his two companions.

A small stone rebounded from rock to rock, then rolled into the sudden silence that followed.

When a long-legged, blue-eyed cat appeared out of the darkness, paused, then filled the clearing with a strident plaintive voice before walking up to the dog and calmly taking a piece of meat from him, the Indians laughed until they were speechless and hiccoughing. The two little boys rolled on the ground, kicking their heels in an abandonment of mirth, while the cat chewed his meat unmoved; but this was the kind of behaviour the bull terrier understood, and he joined in the fun. But he rolled so enthusiastically that the wounds reopened: when he got to his feet again his white coat was stained with blood.

All this time the young dog crouched on the hillside, motionless and watchful, although every driving, urgent nerve in his body

fretted and strained at the delay. He watched the cat, well-fed and content, curl himself on the lap of one of the sleepy children by the fire; he heard the faint note of derision in some of the Indians' voices as a little, bent, ancient crone addressed them in earnest and impassioned tones before hobbling over to the dog to examine his shoulder as he lay peacefully before the fire. She threw some cattail roots into a boiling pot of water, soaked some moss in the liquid, and pressed it against the dark gashes. The old dog did not move;

only his tail beat slowly. When she had finished, she scooped some more meat on to a piece of birchbark and set it on the grass before the dog; and the silent watcher above licked his lips and sat up, but still he did not move from his place.

But when the fires began to burn low and the Indians made preparations for the night, and still his companions showed no sign of moving, the young dog grew restless. He skirted the camp, moving like a shadow through the trees on the hill behind, until he came out upon the lake's shore a quarter of a mile upwind of the camp. Then he barked sharply and imperatively several times.

The effect was like an alarm bell on the other two. The cat sprang from the arms of the sleepy little Indian boy and ran towards the old dog, who was already on his feet, blinking and peering around rather confusedly. The cat gave a guttural yowl, then deliberately ran ahead, looking back as he paused beyond the range of firelight. The old dog shook himself resignedly and walked slowly after – reluctant to leave the warmth of the fire. The Indians watched impassively and silently and made no move to stop him. Only the woman who had first befriended him called out softly, in the tongue of her people, a farewell to the traveller.

The dog halted at the treeline beside the cat and looked back, but the commanding, summoning bark was heard again, and together the two passed out of sight and into the blackness of the night.

That night they became immortal, had they known or cared, for the ancient woman had recognized the old dog at once by his colour and companion; he was the White Dog of the Ojibways, the virtuous White Dog of Omen, whose appearance heralds either disaster or good fortune. The Spirits had sent him, hungry and wounded, to test tribal hospitality; and for benevolent proof to the sceptical they had chosen a cat as his companion – for what mortal dog would suffer a cat to rob him of his meat? He had been made welcome, fed and succoured: the omen would prove fortunate.

INTRODUCTION

I am one of Michael Morpurgo's biggest fans. His books always make me wish I had written them myself! War Horse is no exception. It is the deeply moving story of Joey, a beautiful red-bay foal with a distinctive cross on his nose, whose life has an unpromising start when he is sold to a drunken farmer. Luckily, he finds a friend in Albert, the farmer's son, who gently breaks him in and protects him from his father's brutality. When the farmer demands that Joey be put to work or sold, Albert trains him to pull a plough. It's not enough to save him, though. War breaks out and Albert's father needs money to help his struggling farm. And so, much to Albert's distress, he sells Joey to the army . . .

WAR HORSE

MICHAEL MORPURGO

In the few short weeks before I went off to war I was to be
changed from a working farmhorse into a cavalry mount. It was no
easy transformation, for I resented deeply the tight disciplines of the
riding school and the hard, hot hours out on manoeuvres on the
Plain. Back at home with Albert I had revelled in the long rides along
the lanes and over the fields, and the heat and the flies had not
seemed to matter; I had loved the aching days of ploughing and
harrowing alongside Zoey, but that was because there had been a
bond between us of trust and devotion. Now there were endless
tedious hours circling the school. Gone was the gentle snaffle bit that
I was so used to, and in its place was an uncomfortable, cumbersome

Weymouth that snagged the corners of my mouth and infuriated me beyond belief.

But it was my rider that I disliked more than anything in my new life. Corporal Samuel Perkins was a hard, gritty little man, an ex-jockey whose only pleasure in life seemed to be the power he could exert over a horse. Even the officers, I felt, went in trepidation of him; for he knew, it seemed, all there was to know about horses and had the experience of a lifetime behind him. And he rode hard and heavy-handed. With him the whip and the spurs were not just for show.

He would never beat me or lose his temper with me, indeed sometimes when he was grooming me I think maybe he quite liked me and I certainly felt for him a degree of respect, but this was based on fear and not love. In my anger and unhappiness I tried several times to throw him off but never succeeded. His knees had a grip of iron and he seemed instinctively to know what I was about to do.

My only consolation in those early days of training were the visits of Captain Nicholls every evening to the stables. He alone seemed to have the time to come and talk to me as Albert had done before. Sitting on an upturned bucket in the corner of my stable, a sketchbook on his knees, he would draw me as he talked. "I've done a few sketches of you now," he said one evening, "and when I've finished this one I'll be ready to paint a picture of you. It won't be Stubbs – it'll be better than Stubbs because Stubbs never had a horse as beautiful as you to paint. I can't take it with me to France – no point, is there? So I'm going to send it off to your friend Albert, just so that he'll know that I meant what I said when I promised I would look after you." He kept looking up and down at me as he worked and I longed to tell him how much I wished he would take over my training himself and how hard the

Corporal was and how my sides hurt and my feet hurt. "To be honest with you, Joey, I hope this war will be over before he's old enough to join us because – you mark my words – it's going to be nasty, very nasty indeed. Back in the Mess they're all talking about how they'll set about Jerry, how the cavalry will smash through them and throw them clear back to Berlin before Christmas. It's just Jamie and me, we're the ones that don't agree, Joey. We have our doubts, I can tell you that. We have our doubts. None of them in there seem to have heard of machine-guns and artillery. I tell you, Joey, one machine-gun operated right could wipe out an entire squadron of the best cavalry in the world – German or British. I mean, look what happened to the Light Brigade at Balaclava when they took on the Russian guns – none of them seem to remember that. And the French learnt the lesson in the Franco–Prussian War. But you can't say anything to them, Joey. If you do they call you defeatist, or some such rubbish. I honestly think that some of them in there only want to win this war if the cavalry can win it."

He stood up, tucked his sketchbook under his arm and came over towards me and tickled me behind the ears. "You like that old son, don't you? Below all that fire and brimstone you're a soppy old date at heart. Come to think of it, we have a lot in common, you and I. First, we don't much like it here and would rather be somewhere else. Second, we've neither of us ever been to war – never even heard a shot fired in anger, have we? I just hope I'm up to it when the time comes – that's what worries me more than anything, Joey. Because I tell you, and I haven't even told Jamie this – I'm frightened as hell, so you'd better have enough courage for the two of us."

A door banged across the yard and I heard the familiar sound of boots, crisp on the cobbles. It was Corporal Samuel Perkins passing along the lines of stables on his evening rounds, stopping at each one to check, until at last he came to mine. "Good evening, sir," he said, saluting smartly. "Sketching again?"

"Doing my best, Corporal," said Captain Nicholls. "Doing my best to do him justice. Is he not the finest mount in the entire squadron? I've never seen a horse so well put together as he is, have you?"

"Oh, he's special enough to look at, sir," said the Corporal of Horse. Even his voice put my ears back, there was a thin, acid tone to it that I dreaded. "I grant you that, but looks aren't everything, are they, sir? There's always more to a horse than meets the eye, isn't that right, sir? How shall I put it, sir?"

"However you like, Corporal," said Captain Nicholls somewhat frostily, "but be careful what you say, for that's my horse you're speaking about, so take care."

"Let's say I feel he has a mind of his own. Yes, let's put it that way. He's good enough out on manoeuvres – a real stayer, one of the very best – but inside the school, sir, he's a devil, and a strong devil too. Never been schooled properly, sir, you can tell that. Farmhorse he is and farm-trained. If he's to make a cavalry horse, sir, he'll have to learn to accept the disciplines. He has to learn to obey instantly and instinctively. You don't want a prima donna under you when the bullets start flying."

"Fortunately, Corporal," said Captain Nicholls. "Fortunately, this war will be fought out of doors and not indoors. I asked you to train Joey because I think you are the best man for the job – there's no one better in the squadron. But perhaps you should ease up on him just a bit. You've got to remember where he came from. He's a willing soul – he just needs a bit of gentle persuasion, that's all. But keep it gentle, Corporal, keep it gentle. I don't want him soured. This horse is going to carry me through the war and

with any luck out the other side of it. He's special to me, Corporal, you know that. So make sure you look after him as if he was your own, won't you? We leave for France in under a week now. If I had the time I'd be schooling him on myself, but I'm far too busy trying to turn troopers into mounted infantry. A horse may carry you through, Corporal, but he can't do your fighting for you. And there's some of them still think they'll only be needing their sabres when they get out there. Some of them really believe that flashing their sabres around will frighten Jerry all the way home. I tell you, they have got to learn to shoot straight – we'll all have to learn to shoot straight if we want to win this war."

"Yes sir," said the corporal, with a new respect in his voice. He was more meek and mild now than I had ever seen him.

"And Corporal," said Captain Nicholls, walking towards the stable door, "I'd be obliged if you'd feed Joey up somewhat, he's lost a bit of condition, gone back a bit I'd say. I shall be taking him out myself on final manoeuvres in two or three days and I want him fit and shining. He's to look the best in the squadron."

It was only in that last week of my military education that I began at last to settle into the work. Corporal Samuel Perkins seemed less harsh towards me after that evening. He used the spur less and gave me more rein. We did less work now in the school and more formation work on the open plains outside the camp. I took the Weymouth bit more readily now and began to play with it between my teeth as I had always done with the snaffle. I began to appreciate the good food and the grooming and the buffing up, all the unending attention and care that was devoted to me. As the days passed I began to think less and less of the farm and old Zoey and my early life. But Albert, his face and his voice stayed clear in my mind despite the unerring routine of the work that was turning me imperceptibly into an army horse.

By the time that Captain Nicholls came to take me out on those last manoeuvres before we went to war I was already quite resigned to, even contented in my new life. Dressed now in field service marching order, Captain Nicholls weighed heavy on my back as the entire regiment moved out onto Salisbury Plain. I remember mostly the heat and the flies that day for there were hours of standing about in the sun waiting for things to happen.

Then with the evening sun spreading and dying along the flat horizon the entire regiment lined up in echelon for the charge, the climax of our last manoeuvres.

The order was given to draw swords and we walked forward. As we waited for the bugle calls the air was electric with anticipation. It passed between every horse and his rider, between horse and horse, between trooper and trooper. I felt inside me a surge of such excitement that I found it difficult to contain myself. Captain Nicholls was leading his troop and alongside him rode his friend Captain Jamie Stewart on a horse I had never seen before. He was a tall, shining black stallion. As we walked forward I glanced up at him and caught his eye. He seemed to acknowledge it briefly. The walk moved into a trot and then into a canter. I heard the bugles blow and caught sight of his sabre pointing over my right ear. Captain Nicholls leant forward in the saddle and urged me into a gallop. The thunder and the dust and the roar of men's voices in my ears took a hold of me and held me at a pitch of exhilaration I had never before experienced. I flew over the ground out ahead of the rest of them except for one. The only horse to stay with me was the shining black stallion. Although nothing was said between Captain Nicholls and Captain Stewart, I felt it was suddenly important that I should not allow this horse to get ahead of me. One look told me that he felt the same, for there was a grim determination in his eyes and his brow was furrowed with concentration. When we overran the 'enemy' position it was all our riders could do to bring us to a halt, and finally we stood nose to nose, blowing and panting with both captains breathless with exertion.

"You see, Jamie, I told you so," said Captain Nicholls, and there was such pride in his voice as he spoke. "This is the horse I was telling you about – found in deepest Devon – and if we had gone

on much longer your Topthorn would have been struggling to stay with him. You can't deny it."

Topthorn and I looked warily at each other at first. He was half a hand or more higher than me, a huge sleek horse that held his head with majestic dignity. He was the first horse I had ever come across that I felt could challenge me for strength, but there was also a kindness in his eye that held no threat for me.

"My Topthorn is the finest mount in this regiment, or any other," said Captain Jamie Stewart. "Joey might be faster, and all right I'll grant he looks as good as any horse I've ever seen pulling a milk float, but there's no one to match my Topthorn for stamina – why he could have gone on for ever and ever. He's an eight horsepower horse, and that's a fact."

On the way back to the barracks that evening the two officers debated the virtues of their respective horses whilst Topthorn and I plodded along shoulder to shoulder, heads hanging – our strength sapped by the sun and the long gallop. We were stabled side by side that night, and again on the boat the next day we found ourselves together in the bowels of the converted liner that was to carry us off to France and away to war.

INTRODUCTION

Surprisingly few of Hans Christian Andersen's fairytales revolve around animals, but this one is a classic. Andersen himself was born in 1805 in the slums of Odense in Denmark. His father was a shoemaker, his mother a washerwoman. His father loved literature. He encouraged his son to write and to arrange puppet shows. It wasn't until 1835 that Andersen began to write the fairytales upon which his continuing fame rests. Between then and 1872 he wrote 165 of them, all but a dozen completely original rather than based on traditional folktales. 'The Nightingale' is one of his finest.

THE NIGHTINGALE

HANS CHRISTIAN ANDERSEN
RETOLD BY JENNY KORALEK

This is a story about an emperor of China who was, of course,
Chinese. It happened a long time ago, but it's worth telling
again so it is not forgotten.

The emperor's palace was the most splendid in the world.
It was made entirely of the best porcelain, which was so fragile
that one had to be careful at every step. The most wonderful
flowers grew in the garden. They were hung with silver bells
which rang out when the wind blew. The emperor's garden was
so enormous that even the gardener did not know where it
ended. Beyond it lay deep lakes and a forest which went
right to the sea.

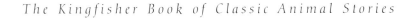

In a tree at the water's edge lived a Nightingale, which sang so beautifully that even the busy fisherman on his way to put out his nets listened to it.

"How beautiful!" he said, each time he heard the bird. "How beautiful!"

Many travellers came from all over the world to visit the city of the emperor, and they admired it very much, and the palace, and the garden, but when they heard the Nightingale, they said, "That is more beautiful than anything else." And when they went home they told everyone what they had seen and some of them wrote books about the Chinese emperor and his city, his palace and his garden; and the ones who were poets wrote fabulous poems about the Nightingale in the woods.

Some of these books found their way to the emperor. He sat in his golden chair and read them from cover to cover. He nodded with pleasure at the excellent descriptions of his city, his palace and his garden. But when he came to the place where it said, "But the Nightingale is more beautiful than anything else," he was puzzled.

"What's this?" he exclaimed. "I don't know anything at all about the Nightingale. Is there such a bird in my own garden? I've never heard a word about this bird. To think I should have to learn such a thing from a book!"

And he sent at once for his Lord Chamberlain who was very grand and had a very high opinion of himself.

"It says in this book that there is a wonderful bird here called a Nightingale!" said the Emperor. "They say it is the best thing in all my great empire, so why have I never heard anything about it?"

"Only because he has never been invited to the palace," said the Lord Chamberlain, who did not want the Emperor to know that he too had never heard of the Nightingale.

"I command that he shall appear this evening, and

sing before me," said the Emperor. "So go and find him!"

"At once, Your Majesty!" said the Lord Chamberlain. "I will go and find him at once!"

But where was he to be found? The Lord Chamberlain ran up and down all the staircases, through halls and passages, but no one had heard of the Nightingale. So he ran back to the Emperor, and said that it must have been made up by the writer of the book.

"But the book," said the Emperor, "was sent to me by the mighty Emperor of Japan, so it cannot be untrue. I will hear the Nightingale! I insist, and I will hear it this very night!"

"Tsing-pe!" said the Lord Chamberlain, and again he ran up and down all the staircases and through all the halls and corridors and this time he met a little kitchen-maid who said, "The Nightingale? Oh yes! It sings beautifully. Every evening I am allowed to take the leftovers to my sick mother. She lives down by the seashore and on my way back I stop for a rest in the wood, and that's when I hear the Nightingale sing. It's so beautiful it always makes me cry!"

"Little kitchen-maid," said the Lord Chamberlain, "if you will lead us to the Nightingale, I will get you permission to watch the Emperor eating his supper!"

Followed by half the Emperor's court the kitchen-maid led the way to the wood. When they were halfway there a cow began to moo.

"Oh!" cried the courtiers. "That's it! That's the Nightingale. Surely we've heard it before."

The little kitchen-maid laughed. "No, those are cows!" she said.

Then the frogs began to croak down by the lake.

"Glorious!" said the courtiers. "It sounds just like church bells."

"No, those are frogs!" laughed the little kitchen-maid. "But now I think we shall soon hear it."

And then the Nightingale began to sing.

"There it is!" said the kitchen-maid and she pointed to a little grey bird up in the boughs of a tree.

"How disappointing!" cried the Lord Chamberlain. "It looks so plain, so dull! It must have lost all its colours at seeing so many important people."

"Little Nightingale!" called the kitchen-maid. "Our gracious Emperor wishes you to sing for him."

"With the greatest pleasure!" replied the Nightingale, thinking that the Emperor was there with the others, and began to sing most beautifully.

"No, no, my excellent little Nightingale," said the Lord Chamberlain. "The Emperor is not here but in the palace; he has sent me to ask you to come and sing for him there this evening."

"My song sounds best out in the open air!" replied the Nightingale, but it agreed to do what the Emperor wished.

That evening the Emperor sat on his throne in the palace with a golden perch at his side for the Nightingale. The whole Court was present, and the little kitchen-maid was

allowed to stand behind the door. Everyone looked at the
little grey bird, and at a nod from the Emperor, the Nightingale
began to sing so beautifully that the Emperor's eyes filled with
tears, which poured down his cheeks. And then the Nightingale
sang more sweetly still, and pierced his heart. He was so pleased
that he offered the Nightingale his golden slipper, but the
Nightingale said, "Thank you, but I have seen tears in your eyes
and that is the treasure. I am rewarded enough!" And then it sang
again with its sweet voice.

From that day the Nightingale lived in the palace. It had its own
cage and was allowed to go out once a day accompanied by
twelve servants, each of whom held on tightly to a silken string
tied to the bird's leg.

The whole city talked of nothing but the wonderful bird, and if
two people met, one said, "Nightin," and the other said "gale," and
they smiled at one another happily. Eleven children were named
after the bird, but not one of them could sing a note and the
ladies at Court even put water in their mouths and gurgled when
they spoke, hoping that they sounded like the Nightingale.

One day the Emperor received a large parcel, on which was
written, "The Nightingale".

It contained a box with a clockwork nightingale in it, which
could sing like the real one. It was made of gold and silver and
brilliantly decorated with diamonds and rubies. As soon as it was
wound up its little silver tail went up and down, and it sang just
like the real Nightingale. Round his neck hung a little ribbon, and
on that was written: "This gift from the Emperor of Japan is a poor
toy compared with the Emperor of China's real bird."

"Oh no!" said everyone. "It's lovely! They must
sing together!"

And so the two birds had to sing together; but it did not

sound very nice, for the real Nightingale sang in its own
way, and the clockwork nightingale sang dance tunes.
But when the clockwork bird sang by itself it sounded just as
good as the real one, and with all those jewels was much
prettier to look at.

It sang the same song more than thirty-three times but was not
tired. The courtiers would have been happy to go on listening
to it but the Emperor said, "No! It's time for the real
Nightingale to sing something now."

But where was it? No one had noticed that it had flown away
out of the open window, back to the green wood.

"Ungrateful bird!" said the Emperor.

"Never mind," said the courtiers. "The clockwork bird is better
and prettier."

So the Emperor banished the real Nightingale from the empire, and put the clockwork bird on a silken cushion next to his bed.

A whole year went by. The Emperor, the Court, and all the people in China knew every little twitter of the clockwork bird's song by heart.

But one evening, when it was singing at its best, something inside the bird broke. It whirred and went "Ping!" and the music suddenly stopped.

The Emperor jumped out of bed and sent for his doctor, but what could he do? Then they sent for a watchmaker, who, after poking about, said that the bird must be carefully treated, for the clockwork pieces were wearing out and it would be impossible to put in new ones. He said the bird could only sing once a year and even that was one time too many.

Five years went by, and the Emperor fell ill. He was not expected to live much longer. He lay cold and pale in his magnificent bed with its long velvet curtains and heavy gold tassels. The window was open, and the moon shone in upon the Emperor and the clockwork bird.

The poor Emperor opened his eyes, and he saw Death standing at the foot of his bed wearing his golden crown, and holding his sword, and in the other hand his beautiful banner. Round him floated strange shadowy faces. These were all the Emperor's bad and good deeds whispering to him about his past.

"Do you remember this?" they whispered. "Do you remember that?"

The Emperor shivered and shook. "Music!" he cried out. "Let me have music so that I cannot hear what they are saying!"

"Sing!" cried the Emperor. "You little precious golden bird, sing, sing!"

But the bird was silent on its golden perch. No one was there to wind him up. Then suddenly through the window came the most beautiful song. It was the real Nightingale sitting on the branch of a tree. It had heard that the Emperor was dying, and had come to sing to him of comfort and hope. And as it sang the shadowy faces grew paler and paler, and the Emperor began to feel stronger. Even Death himself listened, and said, "Don't stop, little Nightingale, don't stop!"

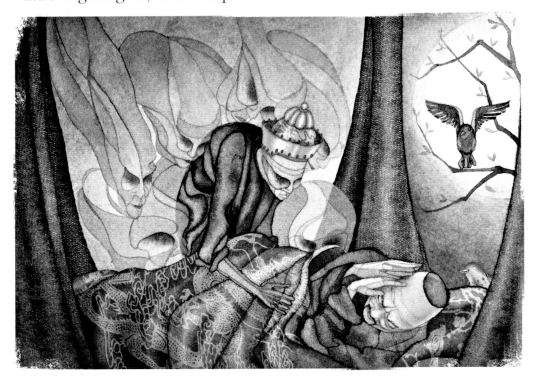

"I'll go on singing if you give me that splendid golden sword, the banner and the Emperor's crown!"

And Death gave up each of these treasures for the love of the Nightingale's song. And the Nightingale sang on and on. It sang of the quiet churchyard where the white roses grow and where the elder blossom smells sweet, and where the grass is wet from the tears of those who mourn. All at once Death felt a longing to see his garden, and floated out of the window in

the form of a cold white mist.

"Thank you! Thank you!" said the Emperor. "You heavenly little bird! I know you well. I banished you from my empire, and yet you have charmed and banished Death himself! How can I reward you?"

"You have rewarded me!" replied the Nightingale. "I drew tears from your eyes when I sang the first time – I shall never forget that. Those are the jewels that rejoice a singer's heart. But now you must sleep and grow strong again. I will sing you a lullaby."

And it sang, and the Emperor fell into a sweet deep sleep. The sun was shining on him through the window when he awoke, completely well again. He was all alone as everyone thought he was dead. Only the Nightingale still sat beside him and sang.

"You must always stay with me now," said the Emperor, "and I shall break the clockwork bird into a thousand pieces."

"No! No!" replied the Nightingale. "It did what it could. Keep it and let me come when I feel the wish. Then I will sit in the evening on that branch by the window, and sing of those who are happy and of those who suffer. I will sing of all the good and of evil that you cannot see. A little singing bird can fly all over your empire and listen to the poorest fisherman and the richest farmer. I will come and sing to you and tell you all I hear – but one thing you must promise me."

"Anything!" said the Emperor, standing there once more in his imperial robes with his gold sword at his side.

"Never tell anyone that you have a little bird who tells you everything." And the Nightingale flew away.

The servants came in expecting to see their Emperor lying dead, but there he stood, alive and well. He turned to them with a smile and said, "Good morning!"

NOTES ON THE AUTHORS

JOY ADAMSON (1910–1980) was a naturalist and wildlife preservationist, best known for her stories about Elsa, her tame lioness. Born in Austria, Joy moved to Kenya in 1938, where she met and married George Adamson. Together, they raised Elsa from a tiny cub, and worked to help many animals, including elephants, buffaloes and leopards. *Born Free* was made into a film in 1966.

AESOP (c. 6th century BC) is believed to have been born into slavery, though the place of his birth is disputed. His master eventually freed him since he was so impressed by the slave's intelligence and wit. More than 600 fables are attributed to Aesop, most featuring animals, and all including a clever moral at the end.

HANS CHRISTIAN ANDERSEN (1805–1875) was born in Odense, Denmark. His family was very poor and he received little early education. He worked as a tailor, a weaver and an actor before returning to school at seventeen. He eventually went to Copenhagen University and began a career as a writer, producing plays, travel books and novels. He is best known for his fairytales and children's stories.

SHEILA BURNFORD (1918–1984) was born in Scotland but emigrated to Canada in 1951. She is best remembered for *The Incredible Journey* (1961) which became a best seller after it became a Disney film in 1963, but she also wrote several other books for children, as well as *One Woman's Arctic* (1973) about Inuit life.

BETSY BYARS is an American children's author who was born in Charlotte, North Carolina in 1928. She began writing for magazines in 1956, and published her first book, *Clementine*, in 1962. A Newbery Medal winner and recipient of both a National Book Award and an Edgar Award, she is also a licensed aircraft pilot. *The Midnight Fox* was first published in 1968.

GERALD DURRELL (1925–1995) was a naturalist, zookeeper, conservationist, author and television presenter. He was born in India, but his family moved to England in 1928 after the death of his father. A move to Corfu in 1935 allowed him to indulge his passion for animals. He wrote several bestselling memoirs about this time, and about his life as an animal collector. He worked tirelessly to help save animals from extinction, and the zoo he founded on Jersey was the first in the world to house only endangered species.

KENNETH GRAHAME (1859–1932) was born in Edinburgh, but following the death of his mother he was sent to live with his grandmother in Berkshire, where he grew up. He worked in the Bank of England for many years, writing essays and stories in his spare time. He created the characters of *The Wind in the Willows* when writing letters to his son, Alastair. The book was first published in 1908.

JOEL CHANDLER HARRIS (1848–1908), an American journalist and folklorist, was born in Eatonton, Georgia. He began writing the *Uncle Remus* tales featuring Brer Rabbit and Brer Fox in 1880. The stories were based on traditional African-American folk tales and were immensely popular in the US following the Civil War. Harris also wrote several collections of stories about life in rural Georgia.

DICK KING-SMITH was born in 1922 in Gloucestershire. He is a prolific children's author, best known for writing *The Sheep-Pig*, upon which the film *Babe* was based. He was a farmer for 20 years before becoming an author, and he loves to write about animals. He has written over a hundred books, which have sold over five million copies in the UK alone and been translated into twelve languages. *The Hodgeheg* was first published in 1987.

RUDYARD KIPLING (1865–1936) was born in Bombay, India. Sent home to England to go to school, he was wretchedly unhappy, but returned to India in 1882 as a journalist, which was the start of his career as an author and poet. He wrote for children and adults and his work includes *The Jungle Book* (1894), *Kim* (1901) and *Just So Stories* (1902). In 1907 he was awarded the Nobel Prize for Literature.

MICHAEL MORPURGO was born in 1943 in St Albans, Hertfordshire. As a child, he was very homesick when sent away to boarding school, and took refuge in reading, particularly poetry. He worked as a teacher but discovered a talent for storytelling, and has written more than a hundred works for children. From 2003 to 2005 he was the Children's Laureate. His books include *The Wreck of the Zanzibar*, which won the Whitbread Children's Novel Award in 1995. *War Horse* was published in 1982 and was adapted for the stage in 2007.

ROBERT C. O'BRIEN was the pen name for Robert Leslie Conly (1918–1973), an American author and journalist for *National Geographic*. Born in Brooklyn, New York, he was interested in both music and literature, but is best known for his children's books, including *Mrs Frisby and the Rats of Nimh* (1971). It won the Newbery Medal in 1972 and was made into a film in 1982.

GEORGE SELDEN (1929–1989) was the pseudonym of the American writer George Selden Thompson, who was born in Hartford, Connecticut. He is best known as the author of several books about the character Chester Cricket and his friends. He wrote more than 15 books in all and two plays. *The Cricket in Times Square* won a Newbery Medal in 1961.

OSCAR WILDE (1854–1900) was an Irish playwright, novelist, poet, and author of short stories. Born in Dublin, he lived in Paris, London and New York as an adult, acquiring a reputation as a wit and becoming an immensely successful playwright. Sent to prison for two years in 1895, he never recovered his health and died in Paris.

LAURA INGALLS WILDER (1867–1957) was an American author who was born near the village of Pepin, Wisconsin. Her accounts of her early life in a pioneering family in Wisconsin, Kansas, Minnesota and Dakota form the nine-book *Little House* series. In 1933, she published *Farmer Boy*, her account of her husband Almanzo's childhood in upstate New York.

URSULA MORAY WILLIAMS (1911–2006) was born in Petersfield, Hampshire. Her twin sister encouraged her to write, and over the course of her career she wrote more than seventy novels for children. Combining fantasy with lively characterisation, books such as *The Adventures of the Little Wooden Horse* (1938) and *Gobbolino the Witch's Cat* (1942) made her famous around the world.

ACKNOWLEDGEMENTS

The publishers would like to thank the copyright holders for permission to reproduce the following copyright material:

Joy Adamson: extract from *Born Free* by Joy Adamson, published by Macmillan. Reprinted with permission of Macmillan. **Sheila Burnford:** Extract from *Incredible Journey* by Sheila Burnford, copyright © 1960,1961 by Sheila Burnford. Used by permission of Bantam Books, a division of Random House, Inc. **Betsy Byars:** 'The Black Fox', from *The Midnight Fox* by Betsy Byars, copyright © 1968 by Betsy Byars, text. Used by permission of Viking Penguin, A Division of Penguin Young Readers Group, A Member of Penguin Group (USA) Inc., 345 Hudson Street, New York, NY 10014. All rights reserved. **Gerald Durrell:** Extract from *My Family and Other Animals* by Gerald Durrell. Copyright © Gerald Durrell 1956. Reproduced with permission of Curtis Brown Group Ltd, London on behalf of the Estate of Gerald Durrell. **Dick King-Smith:** Extract from *The Hodgeheg* by Dick King-Smith published by Hamish Hamilton in 1987. Copyright © Dick King-Smith 1987. Reprinted with permission of A. P. Watt Limited on behalf of Dick King-Smith. **Jenny Koralek:** 'The Nightingale' retold by Jenny Koralek, from *A Treasury of Stories from Hans Christian Andersen* (Kingfisher). Reprinted with permission of David Higham Associates Ltd. **Michael Morpurgo:** extract from *War Horse* by Michael Morpurgo, published by Egmont. Reprinted with permission of David Higham Associates Ltd. **Robert C. O'Brien:** Reprinted with the permission of Atheneum Books for Young Readers, an imprint of Simon & Schuster Children's Publishing Division from *Mrs Frisby and the Rats of Nimh* by Robert C. O'Brien. Copyright © 1971 Robert C. O'Brien; copyright renewed 1999 Christopher Conly, Jane Leslie Conly, Kate Conly and Sarah Conly. **Saviour Pirotta:** 'The Jay and the Peacocks', retold by Saviour Pirotta, from *Aesop's Fables* (Kingfisher, 2005). Reprinted with permission of the author. **S. E. Schlosser:** 'Brer Fox Catches Old Man Tarrypin' retold by S. E. Schlosser copyright © S. E. Schlosser www.americanfolklore.net. Reprinted with permission. **George Selden:** "Tucker's Life Savings" from *The Cricket in Times Square* by George Selden and Garth Williams. Copyright © 1960 by George Selden Thompson and Garth Williams. Copyright renewed 1988 by George Selden Thompson. Reprinted by permission of Farrar, Straus and Giroux, LLC. **Laura Ingalls Wilder:** Text copyright 1933, 1961 Little House Heritage Trust. Used by permission of HarperCollins Publishers. **Ursula Moray Williams:** Extract from *Gobbolino the Witch's Cat* copyright © Ursula Moray Williams 1942. Reprinted with permission of Kingfisher Publications.

Every effort has been made to obtain permission to reproduce copyright material but there may be cases where we have been unable to trace a copyright holder. The publisher will be happy to correct any omissions in future printings.

The publisher would like to thank the artists for their original illustrations as follows:

Paula Bowles: illustrations for *Mrs Frisby and the Rats of Nimh* copyright © Paula Bowles 2008. **Lucy Davey:** illustrations for *War Horse* copyright © Lucy Davey 2008. **Fomina:** illustrations for *Brer Fox Catches Old Man Tarrypin* copyright © Fomina 2008. **Yvonne Gilbert:** illustrations for *Farmer Boy* copyright © Yvonne Gilbert 2008. **Susan Hellard:** illustrations for *The Cricket in Times Square* copyright © Susan Hellard 2008. **Paul Howard:** illustrations for *Gobbolino the Witch's Cat* copyright © Paul Howard 2008. **Richard Johnson:** Illustrations for 'The Jay and the Peacocks' taken from *Aesop's Fables* (Kingfisher 2005) copyright © Richard Johnson. Reprinted with permission of the illustrator. **David Kearney:** illustrations for *The Incredible Journey* copyright © David Kearney 2008. **Adrienne Kennaway:** illustrations for *Born Free* copyright © Adrienne Kennaway 2008. **Sally Anne Lambert:** illustrations for *The Midnight Fox* copyright © Sally Anne Lambert 2008. **Georgina McBain:** illustrations for *The Wind in the Willows* copyright © Georgina McBain 2008. **Elinor Mutale:** illustrations for *My Family and Other Animals* copyright © Elinor Mutale 2008. **Niroot Puttapipat:** illustrations for *The Hodgeheg* copyright © Niroot Puttapipat 2008. **M. P. Robertson:** illustrations for *How the Whale Got His Throat* copyright © M. P. Robertson 2008. **Daniela Terrazini:** illustrations for *The Nightingale* copyright © Daniela Terrazini 2008. **Olwyn Whelan:** illustrations for *The Happy Prince* copyright © Olwyn Whelan 2008.